BRICK BRANNIGAN IS KNEE-DEEP IN PERIL!

BY ERIC BONKOWSKI

DEDICATION

For Kathleen. Thank you for being my adventuress and
heroine. And to Lester Dent and Norvell W. Page for
millions of words and an cternity of inspiration.

BRICK BRANNIGAN IS
KNEE-DEEP IN PERIL!

CHAPTER 1: In Which We Meet Our Wonderfully Illustrious Heroes (and Some Chaos Ensues!)

- The Colony and Protectorate of Nigeria -
- Fall 1935 -

He was sitting in the bed of an old mud-spattered truck, slipping fresh bullets into the six chambers of his .38 when the first explosion sounded in the thick jungle. Doctorate piled on doctorate, he was trained in archaeology, mythology, anthropology, psychology, zoology, geology, chemistry, cryptozoology, psychology, pseudoscience, English, medicine, and world history. He loaded the last bullet into the .38 and slapped the cylinder closed. Academia aside, there were some things you simply could not learn in a classroom.

Hugo "Brick" Brannigan leaned forward and returned the pistol to the holster on his right hip. "Sword of Damocles!" he exclaimed. "I'm too late!"

He was, in fact, too late. The Temple of Aja was now under siege by the terrible forces of Black Fang Delacroix and his Legion of Madmen. The second explosion sounded through the jungle and the scent of nitroglycerine became heavy in the air.

Brannigan rose to one knee and banged on the rear

window of the truck's cabin. "Step on it, Andrew, or all will be lost!"

In the cabin, Andrew Caine–Brannigan's young, pale-faced assistant–shifted gears and bit his lip. Partner of three years, young Caine was one of Brannigan's most loyal friends. What he lacked in skill, Caine more than made up for in courage and zeal. "Aye oh, Professor, sir!"

Ahead, the road curved to the left and inclined, the deep ruts of the roadway leading up the hill towards the crooked stone structure Brannigan knew lay buried in the jungle beyond.

Over the rumble of the old jalopy, Brannigan heard the roar of a diesel engine coming to life. He pulled the .38 from its holster and laid his arm across the roof of the truck for support. "Steady as she goes, Andrew! And come out to meet me head on, you dogs!"

Through the tangle of foliage, the silhouette of a roving black iron beast came into view, accompanied only by the sound of thick tree trunks *crunching* under foot. Brannigan squinted, trying to get a clear look at the contraption, suddenly appearing as if in answer to his demand. The fierce man-made monster erupted from the trees, vines tangled across its horrific grill, great steel treads beneath it leaving dust in its wake where stones had once stood.

Brannigan fired a shot, perfect as always, and saw the spark kick off the hull of the machine where the round caught metal and deflected away harmlessly.

"Lay on, Andrew, and damned be him that first cries enough!"

The old truck dipped, wheels churning through a muddy creek bed as the road curved ceaselessly upwards towards the temple, the monstrous machine shadowing them all the while.

Brannigan unleashed a second shot and a third. Each bouncing ineffectually off the tank without so much as a dent in the fearsome paint. Vines stretched to their breaking point before snapping free of the trees only to be pulled under the tread, revealing a gaping fang-toothed maw painted across the tank's body. The long painted black teeth were all too appropriate, Brannigan thought.

"Black Fang, indeed!" he shouted. "I'll make you toothless, you cur!"

A hatch burst open on top of the bestial machine and a soldier rose from within, a scowl on his face, Aegean captain's hat on his head, and a machine gun in hand to boot. Across his left eye, a black patch was stretched, a jagged scar nearly contained beneath. He lined up the machine gun's sights to his one remaining eye and let loose a flurry of fire.

Brannigan ducked beneath the tattered bed of the truck to the *whiff* of bullets passing overhead.

"A .45 calibre, eh? Fire all you like Von Faust, you will not stop us!"

As if in response, a batch of .45 calibre shot shattered the rear window, raining glass across Brannigan's head. From within, Caine shouted, his voice cracking like a small boy's.

"Push on, Andrew!" Brannigan encouraged.

Rounds collided with the battered truck's frame, chewing through the metal and leaving ragged holes behind. Brannigan raised his body and slipped the long barrel of his revolver over the truck's bed and fired once, neatly swatting the hat from atop Captain Heinrich Von Faust's perfectly bald head.

"The next bullet will greet your frontal lobe, you extraordinary buffoon!" Brannigan hollered.

The Thompson sub-machine gun returned to life, sending Brannigan back beneath the lip of the bed. He ran a hand through his well-oiled hair and straightened his pith helmet. When satisfied, he tidied his bushy sideburns with the tips of his fingers and then combed through the mustache that graced his upper lip *a la souvarov* fashion–a style Brannigan had once heard referred to as "friendly mutton chops."

Nomenclature be damned, .45 calibre gunfire was no excuse for a low-life or disreputable appearance.

"The jungle, sir!" Caine shouted over a spat of gunfire. "It is approaching!"

Brannigan peered above the bed, finding the deep green of jungle looming. The Thompson gunfire stopped, leaving only the twin sounds of diesel engines to fill the would-be silence of nature. Rising to his knees once more, Brannigan smiled. The monstrous machine was receding back into the jungle.

"We gave it the good scare, Andrew my boy! Now onward to the Temple of Aja! We've treasures to liberate from the fierce clutches of evil!"

Turning the roar of diesel into the whisper of a sparrow, an epic cannon-fire burst forth from the jungle as 30.06 shells tore into the jalopy's body like it was made from cork, loosing bits of shrapnel into the air like confetti.

Caine screamed again, this time Brannigan adding a "Hammer of Thor!" to the mix as he ducked his head and covered the peaked pith helmet with his hands.

One terrible 30.06 round ripped through the truck's front left tire. A second buried itself in the old jalopy's engine block, sending a geyser of steam jetting up into the air with a squeal and bringing the diesel to a grumbling halt. Black smoke spewed from beneath the old machine's hood.

The truck ground to an abrupt stop. Brannigan leapt from the bed of the truck in a flash, .38 still in hand, and nearly collided with the gangly body of Andrew Caine as he spilled from the driver's side of the cab and tumbled to the muddy earth.

"Sir, I believe the truck has gone as far as she's capable!" the young man said from his prone position on the ground.

Brannigan took hold of the young man and lifted him to his feet, Brick's six feet and six inches dwarfing young Caine by nearly a foot. He surveyed the steaming hood. "Willing, but no longer able. Poor girl. That is all right. Stand tall, Andrew, we must persevere!" Lumbering forward, Brannigan leaned over the hood of the truck and fired into the jungle, the sound of his pistol lost in the storm of 30.06 fire.

When the roar of the gunfire stopped, Brannigan peered forward into the dark shadows of the jungle.

"There, Andrew my boy! Do you see it?"

Beside Brannigan, young Caine squinted against the blinding sun. "See what, Professor?"

"From the peak of that terrible steel beast! They've mounted some kind of automatic machine rifle!"

"Where, sir?"

The booming cannon-like gunfire returned, sending Brannigan and Caine to their knees in the muddy roadway behind the shelter of one of the jalopy's great wheels.

"That's where!" Brannigan shouted.

5

"We're in trouble, sir!" Andrew said. "And holy Hannah, do you smell that?"

"What? Did you say smell, laddy?"

"Aye, Professor!"

"What the bloody Scottish dagger are you talking about, Andrew?" Brannigan shouted.

"Gasoline, sir!"

Brannigan looked down. Kneeling in the mud, his jodhpurs and knee-high leather boots were wet with a nearly translucent liquid he would have easily mistaken for water. It spread around them in long streams.

"Blast it, my boy, you're right! A bullet must have punctured the gas tank!"

"And by the looks of it, we're trapped, sir."

Behind them, long fingers of gasoline completed a circle, trapping them.

The Professor smiled. "No man bearing a loaded firearm and the will to survive is ever trapped, Andrew!"

Brannigan leaned over the hood of the truck to fire only to pull the trigger on an empty chamber. His hand found the bandolier that crossed over his shoulder. It, too, was empty.

"Blast! So much for axioms!" Brannigan shouted.

On the opposite side of the old jalopy, a spark was thrown when a 30.06 caught a cracked shard of flint rock, half buried in the jungle muck.

The river of gasoline came to life in a mad explosion of fire, raising a deadly wall of flame that encircled our intrepid adventurers!

CHAPTER 2: In Which We Learn That Our Adventurers Are More Skilled Than Most

The old jalopy exploded with all the gusto of one of Black Fang Delacroix's sticks of dynamite, sending a swirling ball of flame rising into the air.

Had Brick Brannigan not hefted young Andrew Caine like the slight man he was and leapt to safety in the nick of time, our two adventurers would be little more than charred fleshy ruins scattered across the jungles of Nigeria. Thankfully, in addition to his extraordinary intelligence, Brick Brannigan is also known for his nigh preternatural reflexes and athletic prowess.

"That was close, Professor!" Caine shouted, wiping his filthy face clean on his khaki shirtsleeve. "Can you put me down now, sir?"

"It was indeed close, Andrew." Brannigan said, dropping his young assistant like a mere toy doll. "Now listen, my boy, we need to get into the cover of the jungle. We're far too exposed here."

"Holy cow pies, at least that other fella's not shootin' at us anymore."

"Von Faust will be back to it again soon enough, *and* with that .45 no less," Brannigan said, nodding. "As sure as Sisyphus struggles, lad."

Over the crackle of flames, the two adventurers could

hear the distant shouts in the coarse German tongue. The voices approached.

"Here they come, Andrew."

"What do we do, sir?"

Brannigan bit his lip and surveyed the land, the muddy road offering little in the way of shelter. His eyes moved over the burning wreckage of the jalopy.

"I've an idea, my boy, but we've got to act quickly!"

***

A pair of young German soldiers, swastikas emblazoned on their uniforms, were the first to round the burning ruins of Brannigan's truck. This proved a fine example of their poor luck.

Neither had any way of knowing the trouble he was in when one misplaced step snapped a hastily-constructed tripwire, detonating the explosive package Brick Brannigan had just built.

"Holy Hannah, Professor! How did you manage that?"

"A simple blade-of-grass tripwire set to ignite a makeshift receptacle of siphoned gasoline, of course! What do you think they teach you in Oxford, Andrew?" Brannigan asked. "Or Harvard, or Cambridge, or... oh, nevermind!"

The package detonated with enough force to clear the way, and one second of distraction was all Brannigan needed. He took off with Caine at his heels, cutting a swift path for the tree line as a the fireball rose into the sky.

Gunfire chased them, but with the cover of smoke and

fire, no bullet found its mark. The two adventurers crashed through the underbrush and rolled down a short embankment, coming to a rest in a dry creek bed a ways down from the road.

"On your feet, Andrew, we've got to get to the Temple!"

"The Temple of Aja, Professor?"

"That's right, lad, the Temple of Aja! If Von Faust can keep us off it long enough for Black Fang to get inside, he'll be able to steal the Eye of Aja. Remember what I told you about that stone, Andrew?"

"No, sir."

"Wings of Icarus, Andrew, do you ever listen to what I tell you? The Eye of Aja–"

A bullet slapped at the crown of Brannigan's pith helmet, overturning the khaki hat and flinging it to the ground. The adventurers looked up to see a squad of soldiers crest at the peak of the hill.

"Onwards with haste, Andrew!" Brannigan shouted as he snatched his helmet from the jungle floor. A salvo of gunfire nipped at their heels as our adventurers turned and ran.

They moved parallel to the road, climbing up the hill that led to the great Temple, seated on its peak like an altar atop a dais. Behind them, the heavy crunch of boots followed, stomping foliage and gaining ground with each passing minute.

Brannigan's great size was generally a gift–in particular when it came to hand-to-hand combat and attracting women, but in regards to jungle stealth, it was far from a blessing. Where young Caine could all but disappear in the shadows of the thick forest, Brannigan's uncanny stature made him quite the target.

Bursting through a thick tangle of barbed reeds, Brannigan pulled Caine behind a thick tree, pausing to catch his breath.

"They're gaining on us, sir," Andrew said in a whisper.

"Indeed they are, my boy, but running without a plan is no plan at all."

"What?"

"What I mean is: we need a plan."

"I thought we needed to get to the Temple of Aja?"

"Of course we do, Andrew, of course we do. But we'll need a better means than just running scared. These soldiers are sure to catch us. And if they don't, their bullets surely will."

Reinforcing his theory, a bullet bore deeply into the tree beside them with a gnawing *zzzzzew*, spitting chips of bark out into the air.

Blood drained from Andrew's face. "Well?" he asked.

Brannigan tipped his recovered pith helmet back on his head and wiped sweat from his brow. "Up," he said. "We must climb."

And climb they did. Andrew went first and Brannigan followed, his burly arms wrapping around the tree trunk with remarkable ease. Together, the two adventurers scuttled up the tree and disappeared into the dark eaves above.

Standing in the crook of a long branch, his great shape protecting young Caine, Brannigan looked down from his vantage on their pursuers below.

Without pause, the squad of soldiers passed at a full gallop, never stopping or even slowing to examine their prey's tracks.

"Hah!" Brannigan said. "Be lost, you wicked villains." He turned to Andrew with a smile. "Now, my boy, onward?"

Together, the two adventurers turned their gaze to the horizon, the tree's great height granting them sight of the Temple of Aja for the first time.

And what a sight it was! It was a grand structure, cut from age-darkened stone and rising nearly three-stories into the sky. The blockish structure was ameliorated by regionally anachronistic arches and columns that rose beneath a huge carved bust of the deity Aja. The jungle had begun encroaching on the temple, vines overtaking much of the structure, but from Brannigan's vantage, the sight was enough to take his breath away.

The image was only sullied by the squads of Nazis circling the temple, to say nothing of the dozens of workers doing their damndest to clear the area of foliage and undergrowth.

"Odin's blood," Brannigan swore. "Those workers are clearing the area." A boom sounded in the distance and a great tree tumbled to the earth. "And with dynamite, no less."

"Is that bad, Professor?"

"Well, Andrew, if we didn't need to sneak in undetected, I wouldn't mind a bit."

"Oh, yes. Right."

Brannigan smiled. "Merely a challenge, my boy. But we won't let that stop us, will we?"

CHAPTER 3: In Which We Meet [Some of] Our Villains, Who Are Sufficiently Dastardly!

Black Fang Delacroix–known to his evil friends as Delacroix and to his evil lady friends as simply Fang– stood on an observation deck built at the crest of a small hill, fists on his hips, dark eyes surveying the progress his Legion of Madmen had made on unearthing the Temple of Aja. Significant progress, he reasoned, but not quite significant enough. He rested his hand on the gilded grip of the scimitar that dangled from his wide leather belt and shouted orders to his Madmen.

They responded as he'd hoped, scurrying off in varying directions like a nest of insects after a particularly large boot had entered the fray. He smiled. Good.

"Herr Delacroix," a heavily-accented voice sounded behind him. "I do believe we have a problem."

Fang glanced over his shoulder to see his second, the bald Captain Heinrich Von Faust. With not even a nod, he turned to face the Temple once more.

"What is it, Captain?"

The one-eyed Nazi scowled–his version of a smile–and said one word, a word that made the hair on the back of Fang's neck stand on end. *"Brannigan."*

"Impossible," he said. "That is simply impossible,

Captain! You must be mistaken."

"I am not, Herr Delacroix. I saw his mustachioed face myself."

Fang sighed. Had he more patience, he would point out that Brick Brannigan did not have a mustache, his facial hair was more than that. Fang knew all too well, considering he saw Brannigan's damnable face in his nightmares. Instead of correcting the Nazi Captain, he simply shook his head. An arch villain simply cannot find good heavies these days, he thought.

"How did he find us, Captain?"

"I do not know, sir."

"You are responsible for my security, no?"

"I am, Herr Delacroix."

"And you promised me that we would seize the Eye of Aja unimpeded, did you not?"

"Yes, Herr Dela–"

"Your services were rendered with gold, were they not? Guaranteeing complete secrecy and security? And from the likes of Brannigan, in particular. This is correct, is it not, Captain?" The tone of Fang's voice grew saltier with each syllable that passed his lips.

Had Von Faust any blood remaining in his pale face, it would have grown paler. Since he didn't, it did not. It was pale enough. "Herr Delacroix, I take full responsibility."

A long moment passed. Fang sighed once more. Known for his foresight and brutality, Fang had already played out the remainder of the scene before he spoke again. Von Faust gulped as Fang turned to face him.

"Bring me your best man, Captain Von Faust."

Von Faust gulped again. "My best man, sir?"

"Yes. Your security competence is bad, is your hearing worse?"

Von Faust turned without another word and shouted to a squad of his men that stood at the tree line, machine pistols hanging at their sides.

"Lieutenant Hesse!"

A tall, lean, blonde man stepped from the line and ran up to the parapet, every motion the paragon of efficiency.

"Yes, Captain."

Von Faust turned to Fang. "Herr Delacroix, this is Lieutenant Edmond Hesse. He is my best man. Smartest, fastest, deadliest. He–"

"That's enough, Captain."

Fang turned to Hesse and smiled, showing off his legendary maniacal grin: every tooth filed to a fine point, the pale white of each tooth's enamel painstakingly stained a deep onyx black.

"Lieutenant Hesse. My name is Black Fang Delacroix. Your Captain has informed me that we have a security breach. Is this correct, Lieutenant?"

Hesse gulped, just as Von Faust had. After an unnaturally long beat, he nodded. "It is correct, sir."

"I imagine you are aware of the contract your legion has with me, are you not?"

Hesse nodded again. "I am, sir."

"And what do you think will happen to this contract now that you have failed? And to your Captain? And to you? And your men?"

Hesse suppressed a shrug, the nervousness seeming to leave his body as his predatory gaze turned to Captain Von

Faust. The faintest hint of a smile found the corner of his mouth. "Disciplinary action, sir?"

Fang continued smiling. "Yes, disciplinary action indeed, Lieutenant." He turned to Von Faust, noticeable beads of sweat running down his forehead.

"Herr Fang–" Von Faust began.

Before he could finish his sentence, the scimitar at Fang's hip was out, slipping from its curved sheath with nary a whisper. The blade passed through the air with a faint whistle before passing through skin, flesh, esophagus, bone, flesh, and a tiny bit more skin.

A head fell to the floor of the viewing platform with a *thump*.

Much to Fang's dismay, it did not roll down the ramp to the jungle floor. He nudged it towards the ramp's edge with his boot. Still not enough. He nudged it again. Finally, it began rolling lazily down the ramp, stopping workers in their tracks. He shook his head. Certainly, the forboding theatrics of a rolling head had not been wasted, he hoped.

The body of Hesse slumped and finally collapsed on the platform, a fair dose of blood running down the ramp and dripping into the already dark soil.

Fang turned to the relieved face of Von Faust. "Captain, that will prove to be either the smartest or dumbest thing I've done regarding your employ. The best case scenario is that now you are motivated at the threat of death and you will no longer fail in your mission. The worst case scenario is that I have murdered the man most likely to succeed at your job once you are... released." Fang took a step to Von Faust and wiped the long blade of his scimitar across the Captain's uniform, cleaning his blade and leaving a long curved trail of blood behind.

"Please, Captain, do not make me regret my decision."

Von Faust nodded, a slow stiff nod. "I won't, Herr Delacroix."

Fang smiled. "Now, find me Brick Brannigan, and bring me his head."

CHAPTER 4: In Which Our Heroes Use Clever Disguises to Accomplish the Impossible & Get Terribly Lucky Thanks To Aging Nitroglycerine

Brannigan was much closer than Fang could have imagined.

Crouched with Caine behind a felled tree, Brannigan surveyed the workers as they raised scaffoldings around the temple's high walls. They worked quickly, and with an air of urgency that was unmistakeable.

"What are they doing?" Caine asked.

"If I had to say, it appears they're looking for... the entrance."

"What?"

Brannigan turned to face his younger partner, resting one thick forearm across his jodhpur-clad knee.

"Legend has it that the Temple of Aja was permanently sealed by the goddess after its completion. It is said that the tribes who built the temple prayed over it, and the deity Aja sealed the temple forever to outsiders in order to protect the holy stone."

"The Eye of Aja?" Caine asked.

"That's right, my boy. The Eye of Aja."

"Look, Professor," Caine whispered, pointing.

A soldier who had been assisting in the raising of a scaffold was looking in their direction, his hand closed around the butt of his machine pistol. Brannigan pulled his young partner below the edge of the downed tree and out of the line of sight. From a tangle of foliage, he snapped the stalk of a wide-leafed plant and held it in front of him as a makeshift mask.

Even for Brannigan, it was a stretch. As expected, it did nothing to deter the guard, his interest apparently too well-piqued.

And yet, perhaps this was just what the Professor wanted. When the young guard was within a few paces, Brannigan lunged!

The young guard didn't stand a chance. Brannigan seized the soldier's rifle with one hand as he planted his other elbow into the man's face to the tune of bones breaking. Before the man had a chance to scream, Brannigan rounded and landed a punch into the soldier's stomach, doubling him over. Without a second thought, Brannigan pulled the unconscious man up and over the downed tree, dropping him beside young Andrew Caine's huddled form.

"By the curse of Arthur," Brannigan said, punching a closed fist into an open palm. "I've got a splendid idea, Andrew!"

***

A few short minutes later, Brick Brannigan emerged from the shelter of the downed tree, fresh Nazi uniform stretched across his broad chest, machine pistol dangling from a shoulder strap.

"What, ho, worker bee!" Brannigan shouted ostentatiously. "Carry that rock faster!"

Scuttling behind him was young Andrew Caine, a slab of stone balanced between his two skinny arms. "Aye, sir, Herr... um, Nazi."

Brannigan stalked across the crowded work area with Caine in tow as a stick of dynamite exploded on the tree line, sending a tall crooked tree tumbling to the earth. Ignoring the blast, the two adventurers rounded the temple, Brannigan leading Caine like an overly demanding foreman as he got the lay of the land.

Up close it was a grand structure, indeed. Taller than Brannigan had originally projected, the walls of the Temple of Aja rose at least forty feet up into the air, the twisted spire and chiseled stone face adding another fifteen or so. Brannigan's eyes moved over the surface of the structure as faceless workers peeled tangled vines from mossy stonework. Aside from empty carvings that probably once held perfectly cut stones of amber and aquamarine, the walls were void of the details he'd expected.

On their third pass of the temple, Brannigan called halt and pointed at the base of the wall where Caine dropped his stone load gratefully.

"Well, Andr–uh, I mean, worker bee, it seems we have a problem," Brannigan said softly.

"Sir?"

"There is, indeed, no door here."

"What next, Professor?"

"Mind your disguise, Andrew!" Brannigan whispered. He raised his voice. "Back to work filthy peasant worker bee!" He took Caine's arm and dragged him away from

19

the temple wall, eyes keen to the the looming form of Black Fang Delacroix, overseeing the site from his observation platform. It seemed as though the arch villain's eyes were following them. Finally, Fang looked away.

"Our luck still lives," Brannigan sighed, turning back to Caine. "The last blight we need is to be discovered at this juncture, Andrew."

"You!" a voice shouted.

Brannigan and Caine halted, eyes snapping forward. Each raised a hand and pointed a finger towards their chest. "Me?" they said in tandem.

"You, large man!" A Nazi soldier approached, a scowl on his face. "What is this?"

Brannigan checked the rank on his borrowed uniform. A rifleman: the German equivalent to a PFC. Bottom of the bottom. He gritted his teeth. "What is what, sir?"

"Your uniform, soldier. What is wrong with your uniform?" The angry face of an Ensign approached, Luger already in hand.

Brannigan looked down, surveying his appearance.

He was appalled. Generally, Brannigan fancied himself a man ready at a moment's notice for either an expedition into the jungles of Papua New Guinea or a drop-in at a White House luxury ball. Not necessarily white tie, but more than presentable with fair warning. At the moment, he was below his usual high standard.

The uniform's shirt was stretched tightly across his chest, buttons pulled taut enough to reveal the hairy pale skin of his chest beneath. Worse were his pants. Pale canvas clung to his calves and thighs, cutting deeply into his skin. Around his waist, his own belt performed small miracles keeping the unbuttonable pants closed, but could not bridge the few inches left bare between his belt and high-rising shirt, nearly exposing his navel.

"Did you steal your uniform from a child?" the Ensign demanded.

"Sir, no sir."

"And what of the Reich's standards, *fahnenjunker*? Do you believe you represent our standards?"

Stumbling over a half-dozen terrible excuses, Brannigan found himself saved by an unplanned dynamite explosion that rocked the site, sending debris raining from the sky. Screams and shouts for help littered the air. The Ensign before them muttered a few muted curses before turning on his heel and hurrying into the fray to assist.

"Saved by the boom!" Brannigan said.

"What happened, sir?" Caine asked, breathless.

"By the Hammer of Thor," he said, punching his open palm. "What do you know about dynamite, Andrew?"

Caine shrugged as Brannigan led him away from the ruckus, the pair of adventurers rounding the temple and stepping into shadows. "It explodes?" Caine ventured.

"Well, you are not wrong. Take a look at that crate," Brannigan said, pointing.

Below the observation platform sat a stained wooden crate, lid pried off and lying beside it in the dirt. Stenciled on the side of the crate was a faded logo.

"What about it, sir?"

"If you take a look, there's a logo stenciled there on the side of that crate. It says 'AECI.' What's interesting is that beneath that logo is a second, much older logo. It's faded and nearly worn away, but it's there. Can you read the second one, my boy? I can. It says 'De Beers.'"

"I don't follow, sir."

"Well, AECI stands for 'African Explosives and Chemical Industries.' It's where I get all my dynamite."

"Oh, of course."

"Well, AECI purchased most of their factories from a company called De Beers not long after the turn of the century. So if that crate still has 'De Beers' printed on it, it's old. Still following?"

Caine gave him an uncharacteristically vacant look. Weapons were not his forte.

"Well, here's where it gets interesting," Brannigan said. "Over time, dynamite sweats, literally releasing its nitroglycerine much like sweat, ergo the name. Anyway, when this happens, the dynamite gets incredibly volatile."

"And sometimes it... explodes?" Color drained from Caine's face.

"It does, indeed, laddy!"

"Oh my."

"Looks like these Nazis saved some bucks buyin' old dynamite, not figuring it would end badly."

"That's no good, Professor!"

Another unexpected explosion rocked the clearing, followed by a third. The Legion of Madmen was now in a lather, running about the clearing like an army of headless chickens. Brannigan and young Caine ran farther from the Temple, searching for cover. Coming to a rest behind a large mound of dirt, Brannigan surveyed the site.

He stroked his mustache, his eyes moving across the great space. Before long, they came to the tree line, finally widening as a smile spread across his face. "It's not any good, Andrew, but sometimes loose dynamite helps in tight situations, eh?"

"I don't follow, sir."

"The only thing you need to follow, Andrew, is me. I've got an idea, so let's go!" He took off towards the jungle, leaving the Temple of Aja, the squad of Nazis, and Fang's Legion of Madmen behind.

CHAPTER 5: In Which Our Heroes Investigate Ancient Sewer Systems–Real or Otherwise– Unaware That There Are Many Dangers!

Brannigan was laughing, a deep throaty laugh that echoed endlessly in the stone well.

Oh, yes, our adventurers were inside a well.

Caine's arms were looped around Brannigan's thick neck and he rode the big man's back like a small child. Without a rope, Brannigan climbed down the thirty or so feet of the narrow well passage by simply bracing his feet on opposite sides of the jagged stone walls and easing downward, one step at a time.

"You see, my boy, if the Nazis hadn't been cheap, they wouldn't have purchased old dynamite. If the dynamite wasn't old, it wouldn't be sweating with such fervor. If the dynamite wasn't sweating with such fervor, the nitroglycerine would not have detonated. If the nitroglycerine had not detonated, we would not have had moved to the east side of the temple. If we'd not moved to the east side of the temple, I wouldn't have seen the mouth of this well! And by the red spot of Jupiter, it was the great solution!"

Caine adjusted his grip, his legs swinging in open

space, the young man too dignified to wrap his legs around Brannigan's waist. "Why the well, Professor?"

"We're in the jungles of southern Nigeria, Andrew. There is water everywhere. The Niger Delta surrounds us." He stopped speaking and held his breath, bracing a thick forearm against the curved wall and lowering his leg down another few feet. Caine squeaked as he shifted on Brannigan's back before the big man took a second step and leveled out once more. "You need only dig a foot or two into the rich soil to hit water. This well makes no sense."

"Yes, sir, you explained that twice already. But why are we climbing *down* it?"

With a sigh, Brannigan released his footholds, dropping the last few feet to the dry dirt floor at the bottom of the well. Far above, the small circle of the well's mouth offered little light despite the bright sunshine beyond. From his pocket, Brannigan pulled a small rattling box of wooden matches. He snapped the phosphorus match on his boot heel, a pale light coming to life in the cool dark chamber.

"Because, Andrew, I believe this false well is the true entrance to the Temple of Aja."

***

Black Fang Delacroix was smiling–never a good sign. He lowered the binoculars from his eyes and turned to speak over his shoulder.

"Captain Von Faust, it seems even I am more capable at your duties than you yourself, sir. What have you to say for your Nth failure today?"

Von Faust adjusted his eye patch, releasing a smattering of sweat from beneath the patch like tears from his dead eye. "Do not concern yourself with Brannigan, Herr Delacroix, I beg. Let my men attend to the good Professor."

Fang turned to Von Faust, once more ready to chide Von Faust for rampant incompetence. Unfortunately, he understood all too well that in locating the hidden entrance, Brannigan had indeed helped Fang cross the terrible fjord previously separating him from the Temple of Aja. He chose a different tact. "Now that Brannigan has been detected, why does he still breathe, Captain?"

Von Faust smiled. "The afternoon is young, Herr Delacroix. I ask your continued patience. The good Professor does not have much time left."

Fang nodded and turned back to the temple. "See to it that he is killed. And bring me the Eye of Aja, or I will take your eye in its place. You understand what is at stake."

"The Eye will be yours, sir. The Eye of Aja, that is."

Fang smiled. "I hope so, Monsieur Von Faust. For your sake."

***

Brannigan and Caine stood in a large chamber, the sound of exploding dynamite reverberating through the stone ceiling above and echoing around the room like rumblings of thunder.

"Now what, Professor?"

Brannigan scratched his muttonchops and tipped his pith helmet back. Even in the cool air of the dark chamber, he was sweating.

Two doors faced them, large stone doorways trimmed with gold and precious gemstones. In comparison to the Eye of Aja, Brannigan knew these gemstones were essentially worthless.

"It's a test, Andrew. Of course." He lit another match–his supply dwindling–and walked to the first door. A metal ring was set into the stone, large and smooth. Perfect for pulling, he thought. The second door had a matching ring. Above each ring was a circular disc set into the door, a faint coloring of crimson present on the old stone. An ancient button, as it were.

"Only one of these doors will lead forward, sir?"

Brannigan nodded his head. "Press a button and pull," he said. "Do you remember when I told you about the Niger Delta, Andrew?"

Caine shook his head. "Only that we were in the heart of it."

"We are indeed, my boy, and I've heard legends about deified temples in the Niger Delta. Legends of something French explorers and imperialists used to call *portes de l'eau*, and considering how close we are to the Niger River, herself, this makes me quite worried."

Caine stepped forward to Brannigan's side. "*Portes de l'eau?*" he asked.

"Quite simply, it means 'water doors.'" Brannigan ran his hand along elaborate carvings that decorated the first door. To Caine, the symbols were nothing more than letters of the cyrillic alphabet, albeit of the more exotic variety. He hoped Brannigan's numerous academic degrees proved up to task.

"In chambers like this found in similar temples of the

Niger Delta, there were traps laid behind doors not unlike this one; traps created to protect the very temples they seemed promised to yield."

"So these doors are traps?"

Brannigan turned to Caine and smiled. "*One* of these doors is a trap. Or, as our Monsieur Fang Delacroix would say, Andrew: *une de ces portes est une porte de l'eau.*"

"And if we open that door?"

Brannigan blew out the match and turned over his shoulder, gesturing at the faint glow of light at the end of the far corridor emanating from the mouth of the well. "The water will rush through the open doorway faster than we could possibly hope to react, filling this chamber from here to the well until the pressure equalizes between this room and the source of the water–most likely a tributary of the Niger–drowning us in the process."

Caine gulped. "Drowning us, sir?"

Brannigan nodded. "Yes. Well, to be frank, once the locking mechanism on the incorrect door is released, I will most likely be crushed to death by the door itself. You see, when the water is loosed, the door will be pushed open with a magnificent force, and I am relatively certain I will be killed instantly." He turned to Caine. "You, however, will drown."

"Oh. All right."

Brannigan walked to the second door, lighting a match. Little did Caine know it was his last. He squinted at the carvings and the stone, eyes moving over each symbol slowly. After a moment, he returned to the first door and did the same, the faint flame of his match dwindling.

"All right, Andrew. I believe I've deciphered the runes here and I am quite comfortable that I am correct–"

"Um, Professor..."

"–I am fully confident in my powers of translation, anthropological deciphering, decryption, and of course, educated guesswork–"

"...maybe we shouldn't..."

"–and I have no doubt that the *second door* is the trap!"

"...what if you're wrong, Professor?"

Behind our two adventurers, the first of Von Faust's Nazi agents touched down at the bottom of the well. Silently, he released his repelling rope and stepped into the chamber, raising his automatic rifle.

"Wrong, Andrew? Have I ever been wrong? Now, setting aside the Easter Island manuscript debacle, the Tibetan apocalypse misunderstanding, and not quite hearing the Kremlin diplomat correctly about his vendetta, I do not make mistakes, remember?"

"But sir–"

"But nothing, my boy. The Temple of Aja lies just behind this door," he said, pointing to the right doorway.

Brannigan grasped the stone ring and prepared to pull. Behind him, a trio of Nazis raised submachine guns as Brannigan pushed the crimson button, releasing the lock.

The door opened, releasing the fury of the Niger River herself.

CHAPTER 6: Considering Our Adventurers Are Most Certainly in Mortal Danger, Let's Move to a Much Less Stressful Situation on the Other Side of the Globe. (Less Stressful, Dear Reader, But Only for the Moment)

Doctor Liliana Halifax was wiping a wet dust rag across her broad oak desk. She did it at the end of each day shortly before leaving for home. A knock on her door tugged her attention away from the damp cloth.

"Yes?"

The door opened. Allison Peters, loyal administrative assistant at Branford University peeked her head inside. "Excuse me, Doctor? Do you have a moment to sign for a parcel?"

Dr. Halifax wiped her hands on a second cloth, a dry cloth, and stood upright. She exhaled patiently and straightened her blouse. "A parcel, Ms. Peters?"

"Yes, Doctor. A small package was received from very far away, from the African continent. It was sent by..." Ms. Peters paused dramatically. "...Dr. Spooner."

"Dr. Spooner?" Her breath caught in her throat. Dr. Halifax had heard Ellis Spooner's name before–mentioned only scandalously and in hushed tones–at the first faculty party she'd attended in the fall. She'd come to learn the name Spooner was shrouded in nothing short of infamy.

"Where is Dr. Spooner? Is he still–"

"–missing, yes ma'am."

"I think 'on sabbatical' is the official position."

Dr. Halifax weighed her options. Two and only two options as she saw them: she could examine what promised to be a strange and controversial parcel sent by a strange and controversial faculty member–a man who maintained tenure based solely on ten year-old exploits and a smattering of blindly lucky discoveries in desolate jungles and deserts across the world–an examination that possibly threatened her young reputation and younger tenure; the alternative involved simply denying the package that had traveled so many miles to find its way to her sunny office. She knew very well that no other faculty members remained in the building to sign for a package at this time of day. She also knew that had the whole of the archaeology department remained, not a single faculty member would offer their signature–even for a bribe.

Dr. Halifax weighed the risks versus the rewards, taking well into account that her lack of understanding on this Dr. Ellis Spooner did not automatically translate into his innocence or misunderstood eccentricity; the other faculty members could well be correct in their supposition that he was truly a madman. So that was a check in the 'no' column. And yet, she freely admitted to herself that despite her cautious side, she had made a resolution at the prior winter's Kankakee College New Year's Eve ball to take more risks; melodramatic, she knew–damn the bubbly. Her only true risk so far that year had been to accept tenure at the Quincy Max Institute of the prestigious Branford University. Her unexpected acceptance forced her to pack up and move north, abandoning her friends and family–to say nothing of her cushy research position–back in Kankakee. Not another risk to speak of. Not one. A less interesting person may say that was enough risk for the year.

She looked up at Ms. Peters and said, "Where do I sign?"

***

After accepting the clipboard and paper now bearing Dr. Halifax's fresh signature, Allison Peters placed a small package wrapped in butcher paper and tied with a piece of twine into Dr. Halifax's waiting hands. That accomplished, Ms. Peters crossed the cramped office once more, stepping over meticulously packed boxes rife with books, papers, and well-polished silver fountain pens, and exited.

"Thank you, Ms. Peters," Dr. Halifax said. The door closed behind her with a quiet click.

The thought of continuing her unpacking now gone from her head, Dr. Halifax rested in the creaky wooden desk chair, her rich chestnut eyes appraising the stained, red ink-stamped label borne on the flat face of the parcel.

TO: BRICK BRANNIGAN, it said. **C/O Branford University Archaeology**.

Brannigan. She knew that name. Just across the hall from Dr. Halifax's office was a matching door, the opaque window set into the upper third bearing a stencil reading, "Dr. Hugo Brannigan, Professor and Assistant Dean."

But what was this 'Brick' business?

She snipped the twine and tore through the butcher paper, peeling it back with satisfying rips, revealing a

32

course red leather package within. Whatever it was was held bound by the leather, long strips wrapped tightly around something protectively tied with matching red leather rope. Dr. Halifax slipped a pocket knife from her desk drawer and sawed through the rope. Carefully, she unwrapped the red leather sheath.

In her hands, lying in the open red leather nest was a flat rounded disc cut from the finest black stone. Onyx, Dr. Halifax supposed. It was thin, but seemed to have impressive tensile strength. She dropped the leather onto her desk and turned in her chair, extending the disc into the dying sunlight.

The black stone was flawless, unlike any geological sampling she'd ever before encountered. About the size of a 45 record–only with no hole cut in its center, the disc seemed a perfect circle, although its size and shape were far from its most remarkable quality. That was saved for the inscription carved perfectly into the face of the disc.

She recognized it immediately: Sumerian text. Shapes and glyphs far from the Latin or Greek alphabet, even the Arabic alphabet. The complex array of shapes and minuscule cuneiforms that covered the face of the disc were far closer to the hieroglyphics of Egypt.

Outside, the sun began dipping below the nearly bare branches of the maple trees. Winter was coming. She sighed, slipping a pair of reading glasses on her nose and turning away from the window. She didn't notice the grey Ford pull up in the institute's empty parking lot. Nor did she notice the four men clad in dark trench coats pile out as the engine sputtered to a halt. Nor did she notice the guns in their hands.

With the light failing, Dr. Halifax rose, carrying the onyx disc with her, and stepped out into the hall. She headed towards the kitchenette for a cup of coffee. Her evening had just gotten a lot longer.

CHAPTER 7: In Which Our Heroes Learn the Virtues of Good Swim Technique (Never To Be Overlooked!)

The water was filthy, brown, and bubbling, and it exploded over Brannigan like an avalanche. Fortunately for him, he was wrong when he said that he would be killed instantly by the pressure of the door hitting him full blast. Unfortunately, he was left to tread water along with young Andrew Caine, and tread water for his life.

Behind them, the Nazis didn't even have a chance to get a shot off, much to their collective fascist chagrin.

Brannigan did his damndest to shout words of advice or encouragement to Caine (two of his favorite past times, especially in the midst of an adventure) but a mouthful of water silenced him all too effectively. He was swept from his feet, arms pinwheeling in an effort to get a hold on Caine, his pith helmet blown from his head like a leaf in the wind. Despite his nigh superhuman speed, he was not fast enough.

The water had hit young Andrew Caine at a glancing blow, spinning him backwards and carrying him towards the other doorway–the true entrance to the Temple of Aja, in this case. Brannigan, on the other hand, was thrown straight backwards towards his Nazi foes and the mouth of the well. Even in the large chamber, by the time he slammed into the small squad of pursuers, the water was three foot high and rising.

He kicked, as much against the water as his band of Nazi hunters. He felt his boot hit something solid–but not *too* solid–and the kick was accompanied by a muted shout. A split second later, Brannigan collided with the soldiers in earnest, tangling with the gangly young men in a twisted nest of limbs. Before he knew it, they crashed into the stone wall, a field of stars exploding in Brannigan's eyes.

Caine caught hold of a jagged outcropping on the otherwise smooth stone wall, bringing his swirling trip to a halt. Around him, the water rose. He gripped the wall and began to climb, struggling to keep his chin above the waterline.

From the open maw of the *porte de l'eau*, long reptilian bodies slid, gliding along the surface of the rushing brown water like deadly slices of driftwood.

"CROCS!!" Brannigan shouted, his sopping mustache just peeking over the churning water. "Climb, Andrew!"

Higher and higher it rose, the room a din of rushing water and hoarse, shouting voices.

A machine rifle came to life, the dripping barrel breaking the water's surface like the black head of a snake. Added to the rushing water, the sound was almost deafening. Dust and shards of stone fell from the ceiling.

Kicking his legs, Brannigan closed on the nearest Nazi, the young soldier brandishing the rifle with such an undiscerning eye. The young blonde man lowered the barrel, leveling the rifle at Brannigan's forehead, a pair of blue eyes wide with fear. His fascist finger, invisible beneath the filthy water, had no time to tighten on the trigger. Brannigan cracked a boulder-sized fist into the man's face. A second fist followed. His eyes rolled back into his head as the young man slid beneath the muddy surface, but not before Brannigan liberated the machine pistol from his evil clutches.

Turning his attention back, Brannigan's eyes found Caine clinging desperately to the far wall, thin arms and legs shaking in effort to keep him above the water. As the seconds ticked by, his remaining real estate was shrinking. Only a few feet of wall remained above water.

"Professor!" Caine shouted. "Look!"

Finger shaking, Cained pointed at the pair of long, sleek, black-scaled bodies that moved towards him.

"I see them, Andrew! Get ready to jump, my boy!"

"Jump, sir?"

"Jump!"

Branningan pedaled his legs to stay above the water, aligning the barrel of the machine rifle with the surface of the water, and squeezed the trigger. The gun came to life, spewing rounds through the bubbling Niger and into one of the crocodiles until the gun clicked empty. The beast's mouth opened, bragging a full set of razor-sharp fangs, and increased its speed three-fold. Brannigan dropped the rifle and brandished two tightened fists.

Caine watched helplessly as the crocodile's jaws closed on Brannigan.

Grateful are we, dear reader, that Brick Brannigan has wrestled alligators before. And as we all know, other than snout width, disposition, international geographic proclivities, and teeth visibility, not much distinguishes our close reptilian friends.

One hand closed over the crocodile's broad nose and the second on the substantial chin of the beast's lower jaw, Brannigan struggled, teeth grit, holding the monster's mouth open.

"Professor!!" Caine shouted.

Through his clenched teeth, Brannigan said, "Get ready to jump, Andrew!"

The crocodile writhed against Brannigan's grasp, the muscles in the big man's legs beggining to burn against the swirling current. A half-dozen soggy paces from Brannigan's floating fight, the bubbling surface of the water broke to the form of another fair-haired fascist. From below the surface of the water, a long-barreled Luger rose, hammer drawn back.

Still busy with our croc friend, Brannigan was now defenseless against the Nazi's steel. The soldier pulled the trigger.

The round clicked hollow. Misfire, wet powder, or an empty clip, Brannigan neither knew nor cared. From his belt, the soldier pulled a long serrated blade and approached Brannigan with murder in his eye.

Any other fascist may think twice before getting between Brick Brannigan and a crocodile. Apparently we were dealing with quite an industrious Nazi. Although perhaps he was simply an optimist. Or stupid.

Around the same time, two things happened: Andrew Caine ran out of climbing room, his thin body forced to bend to stay above the water; and the second croc decided to throw his proverbial hat into the ring.

The beast surfaced, two hungry yellow eyes locking on Brannigan.

"Sword of Damacles!" Brannigan shouted. He raised his eyes. "Ready to jump, Andrew?"

"Waiting for the word, Professor!"

The Nazi within a few feet to his left and the second croc within a few feet to his right, Brannigan made his play. Twisting his body and using the croc's body weight against it, he used his nigh superhuman strength to leverage the croc aross his body to his left, slamming the giant reptile into the Nazi with a wet *SMACK*. He released the beast's jaws and let them close with the fury of a maneating mousetrap across the Nazi's chest. Twisting, he seized the young man's wrist and pulled the long blade from his hand.

The second crocodile struck, body shooting through the muddy water like a torpedo. Brannigan swung downward, the deadly blade disappearing into flesh between the crock's two yellow eyes. A slither of blood leaked free.

Slowly, the huge body slipped below the surface of the water. From behind him, Brannigan heard a thrashing in the water. He kicked toward Caine, realizing it was either a Nazi being eaten by a crocodile, a third crocodile, or a second Nazi. Regardless, Brannigan did not stop.

"Jump, Andrew!" Brannigan shouted as an automatic rifle came to life behind him. Round after hot metallic round passed over his head. Angry German rantings followed a moment later.

Caine's flailing body hit the water a moment after Brannigan dove below the surface.

In the dark and muddy water, Brannigan's visibility was reduced to scant inches. It didn't slow him. In a split second, one hand was closed tightly over the other door's ring, his other hand slammed into the crimson stone lock release with all the force of a freight train.

Bracing his boots against the uneven stone wall, Brannigan closed both of his huge hands over the ring and pulled, pushing off the wall with everything he had.

It barely budged. He tried again, mouth opening in a soundless holler of exertion, words lost in a churning of bubbles. The door opened an inch, water slipping through the gap and pulling the doorway shut again with a fiersome force.

Brannigan surfaced, gasping for air. Young Andrew Caine was a moment behind.

"I need your help, Andrew!" Brannigan shouted over persistant rifle fire. "Get beside me and pull with everything you have! The only way out of here is through that door."

Behind our adventurers, the poorly-trained Nazi unleashed another hail of gunfire, hitting nothing but the chamber walls.

"Ready?"

"Yessir, Professor!"

Our two heroes dove, returning to the door in a flash, four hands closing over the door's ring, four legs bracing against the door frame, and two men pulling with all the gusto they could conjure.

The door opened. With every inch it got exponentially harder, but our heroes would not relent. Water rushed through the widening gap, sliding past young Caine and Brannigan like the gale of a hurricane.

When it was wide enough, Brannigan pulled Caine's hands free and the young man was pulled through the gap like a piece of flotsam. A moment later, the huge muscular shape of Brick Brannigan rushed through with the stream of filthy water.

The pressure and power of the water pulled the door closed behind him, but not before a barrel-chested and scar-faced crocodile slipped through.

The entrance slammed behind them with a resounding *BOOM*, the sound echoing through the chamber like thunder.

As the water drained away, our two heroes were left standing on a dais beneath a massive carved statue of the face of Aja. Surrounding it, a cache of treasure, gold pieces and precious stones rose dramatically like a mountain.

Behind them, the crocodile hissed, jaws open wide.

"Yes, indeed!" Brannigan shouted victoriously. "It *is* quite impressive!" He turned to young Caine. "I give you... Aja!"

CHAPTER 8: Before We Explore the Treasures of Aja, Let Us Return to the Prestigious Quincy Max Institute as Trouble Begins...

There was a man in the hallway when Dr. Halifax finished in the small kitchen. Mug of steaming coffee in hand, she pulled the door closed behind her and stopped.

He was standing in the center of the narrow hall, hands buried in the deep pockets of his trenchcoat. Tall and heavyset, the man had dark circles beneath darker eyes.

"Dr. Halifax, I presume?"

"Yes." She took a few steps towards him, but stopped when he didn't step out of her way.

"You can call me Mr. Smith."

Dr. Halifax nodded, but did not speak. Encouraged in some measure, he continued.

"Your office," he said. "It's locked."

"That seems more my concern than yours."

She began to step past him before he moved to block her path once more.

"Where is it?" he asked.

She looked at the mug in her hands. The disc, she realized, she'd left in the kitchenette.

"Where is what?"

He smiled. Thick-lipped and doughy, when Smith smiled he looked more like a pleased pig than a nefarious heavy. In that moment, Dr. Halifax decided she did not like Mr. Smith. She was equally inclined not to help him. In a not-so-mysterious moment of women's intuition, Halifax realized she was in trouble. Real trouble.

"You know, we were running late today, me and my boys. I say 'we' because there are three other men here with me. One at the stairwell at the end of the hall behind me, one at the stairwell at the end of the hall behind *you*, and one at the front door. Anyway, as I was saying, we were running late today. Traffic, you know. Had we *not* run late, this would have been easier, for you at least. You see, at the entrance to State Road 54, we intercepted the express mail truck. The driver's name was Henry. Was. Very cooperative was our young Henry—which helped him in the end, in some measure at least—and he told us he had made his final delivery of the day. As it happens, Henry's last delivery was here at the Quincy Max Institute."

Dr. Halifax's hand tightened on her mug. In her chest, she could feel her heart beating like a drum. She remembered the delivery man. So his name was Henry. Halifax had previously seen him speaking with Ms. Peters. He was young and handsome, freckled and in a rush, most likely to get home. Perhaps he was intersted in Ms. Peters; perhaps he had a girlfriend; perhaps he had a wife. "His name... *was* Henry?" she asked.

Mr. Smith either did not hear her question or simply ignored it. "Had the traffic on Highway 7 not been heavier than expected, we would have met Henry when he was going the other direction on 54, when he was heading *to* the prestigious Quincy Max Institute."

"What do you want?" Dr. Halifax asked.

Mr. Smith smiled piggishly. "You're a doctor, you tell me. I figure you went to a lot of school if you teach here. It's prestigious, you know. You're probably pretty smart."

Dr. Halifax did not answer.

"What do you teach?" he asked.

"I have degrees in archaeology, anthropology, and world history. I... I was brought on to help out in a number of capacities."

Smith smiled again. "You got PhDs and all that?"

"Two," she said. She decided not to recount her masters degrees. Although perhaps she should have. If this was her version of stalling for time, it was a shoddy effort.

"Yeah, of course you do. So tell me, *Doctor*, why do you think I'm here? Considering I been telling you about Henry and all."

"You say this man... Henry? You say he's a delivery man?"

Smith nodded. "He was."

"And he came here?"

"He did."

"Did he deliver a package? I believe the mail room is downstairs, Mr. Smith."

"It is that, Doc. Problem is, they close at 4."

She forced a laugh and awkward smile. "This is a large institute, Mr. Smith."

"Yes, it is."

"Whatever package you are searching for could have been delivered to any department on any floor. Why are you here, Mr. Smith? What do you think I can do for you?"

44

Mr. Smith smiled. "Come now, Doc, you got all those degrees..."

Dr. Halifax let his words settle, taking a sip from her steaming coffee, her hand trembling slightly. When Smith did not continue speaking. She said, "Mr. Smith, I have received no packages today."

"Doctor? *Doctor*?"

Halifax lowered her hands, holding the mug between them so as not to show her fear.

"Yes Mr. Smith, yes. I have received no packages today. All day."

He smiled once more and made a *tssk tssk tssk* sound. At the far end of the hall, Halifax saw the looming form of one of Smith's partners, appearing for the first time.

Slowly, Smith withdrew a meaty hand from one of his pockets. Halifax felt her body tense, knowing full well she had nowhere to run. She waited for the dark metal of the revolver, waited for the *click* of the hammer as Smith pulled it back.

Instead of a *click*, she heard the *crinkle* of paper. Smith extended it to her.

"Is this your signature, Doc?"

She took another sip of her coffee.

"Doc? This ain't no rhetorical question. You see this scribble? Next to where Henry printed 'L. Halifax'? That's you, ain't it?"

"Mr. Smith?" Halifax asked, doing her best version of coy.

"Yeah, Doc?"

She threw the steaming coffee into his beady eyes, steam kicking up off his fat face accompanied by the sizzle of burning skin. Smith screamed and raised his beefy hands to his face. Halifax followed up with the heavy ceramic mug a second later, shattering it across his scorched face.

Dr. Halifax turned and ran back down the hall towards the kitchenette, the heavy sounds of footsteps beating a trail behind her. At the opposite end of the hall, she saw the second of Smith's partners. He was running towards her at full tilt. From his pocket, he pulled a pistol and raised it in her direction.

Halifax slipped into the kitchenette and slammed the door behind her, flipping the lock. The heavy impact of a body came a second later, sending a long crack running down the center of the wooden door.

Halifax turned, grabbing the refrigerator and pulling, overturning the heavy contraption and toppling it to the floor in front of the doorway with a crash. A second impact sounded against the door, the crack worsening. Turning her back to her only exit, Dr. Halifax returned to the tidy countertop and the mysterious onyx disc lying beside the sugar jar.

She picked it up, eyes moving over it in the kitchenette's pale light. *What is this disc?* She thought. *And what has it gotten me into?*

Another crash slammed against the door, this time accompanied by the splintering of wood.

"Oh Doctor..." Smith's voice sounded through the quickly diminishing door. *"Doctor..."* His voice was ragged and desperate with pain. "You have something I want..."

Outside in the hall, the two heavyweights that stood on either side of Smith had their guns in hand. One fired a shot through the door, leveling the blast at the hinges. The second man aimed for the lock.

"It's in my office!" they heard shouted from within. "The package! Just leave me alone!"

The junior heavies turned to Smith, his face scorched red and blistering from the Doctor's coffee. "Check it," he said waving his hand dismissively. "Break the door down if you need to. I'll see to the good Doctor."

The two men disappeared down the hall as Smith pulled a .44 from his coat and slammed the butt against the door. Wood splintered and fell in shattered pieces into the kitchenette. He hit it again and more fell into the room, clattering onto the tile floor.

"I'm looking forward to getting my hands on you, Doctor," Smith growled. "I owe you one for that cup of coffee." He raised his leg and jammed the heel of his foot against the door. The refrigerator bucked against the impact. He kicked again and the appliance slid back far enough to allow him to slip inside. Smith sucked in his gut and entered the kitchenette.

It was empty. The window in the corner was open, curtains blowing in the late fall evening.

Mr. Smith swore loudly, slipping his pistol into his coat. His partners appeared at his back a moment later and reported their findings: nothing.

"Get on the wire," Smith said. "Put out a telegram to the Cabal. The Cipher of Dumuzid has escaped our grasp. But not for long."

CHAPTER 9: In Which Our Heroes Discover Treasures Beyond Your Wildest Dreams and Learn the Perils of, Well, Peril

A mosaic of rubies and emeralds were constructed surrounding onyx orbs, together forming what amounted to a pair of great bright eyes set into the huge face of Aja that governed the room. Dripping wet, Brannigan and Caine began crossing the room, footfalls echoing through the massive space. Behind them, their crocodile follower slipped into the deep moat surrounding the broad dais on which they stood.

"It's amazing," Caine said, his jaw hanging open.

"It is indeed, Andrew! It is indeed."

"The Eye, Professor, which is *the* Eye?" Slowly, he raised a hand and pointed at the jeweled eyes.

"Neither, young Andrew. The eye itself is a single stone, pure and flawlessly cut by nature herself."

Our adventurers boots slapped down against the gold coins, goblets, and open chests of precious gems and treasures that covered the open space. Fifteen feet from the face of Aja, Brannigan extended an arm and stopped Caine in his tracks.

"Wait," he said softly. "How could I have been so careless?"

"What is it, Professor?"

"Sword of Damocles," Brannigan said. "This temple, it's booby trapped to all hell and back. Each step could very well be our last."

Caine's eyes widened, the color draining from his dripping-wet face. "Sir?"

Brannigan smiled. "Nothing to worry about, Andrew. Just follow my lead."

***

Had Black Fang Delacroix been new to 'the business,' he may have been surprised that his best laid plans were currently smoldering ruins. Unfortunately, along with his *evil purpose* and zeal, Fang's ability to be shocked had long since fallen by the way.

"Brannigan escaped, didn't he?" Fang said to Von Faust. He may have raised his voice at the end of the sentence, but it wasn't much of a question.

"Yes, Herr Delacroix." Von Faust was examining his well-polished boots as the two men stood on the observation platform. "In the subterranean chamber, apparently there were two doors."

"*Portes de l'eau,*" he said, shaking his head. "But Brannigan would know that."

"From what I have learned, he opened a door that unleashed a huge stream of water–"

"The Niger," Fang shook his head. "Of course. Of *course!*"

"The room was flooded and Brannigan escaped."

"You seem to be skipping a few steps Von Faust," Fang

said bitterly. "Escaped where?"

Von Faust cast a look over his shoulder at the sopping wet Nazi soldier standing behind him, perhaps the only person looking more sheepish than Von Faust himself. The wet Nazi muttered something.

"A, eh, the second door, Herr Delacroix." Von Faust looked at the sheepish Nazi again. "Brannigan slipped through the second door prior to the chamber completely flooding."

Fang looked up, leveling his wicked eyes on Von Faust. From the officer's belt, he pulled Von Faust's Luger and shot the sopping Nazi soldier, the bullet burying itself in the young man's heart. He collapsed with little ceremony.

Fang squeezed the gun butt and clenched his teeth. After a long moment, he lowered the pistol once more. He stared into Von Faust's eyes and searched for words, a bigger and better threat that would somehow capture that maddening frustration he was feeling. Unfortunately, he could muster no words for that much frustration.

"Dynamite, Captain," he said finally. "Bring the dynamite and lay it on the southeastern walls of the temple. If there is, in fact, no door, we shall create a door. And if you really are as stupid as you are trying to convince me that you are, Captain, then you will no longer make decisions. You will simply follow *my* orders. Bring the damned dynamite. I want the southeastern wall to be nothing more than a smoking hole in the next five minutes. If it takes six minutes, Captain, please return to me here at the observation platform." Fang pulled back the hammer on the Luger, the pistol clicking loudly. "I have something here I'll need to give you."

***

The dais more resembled a cube surrounded by a moat than anything else. Languidly circling the muddy water in the moat was the crocodile that had followed Caine and Brannigan through the entrance. On the dais and beneath our adventurers' feet, mountains of gold and treasures shifted unsteadily with each step. After Brannigan's realization, they had not moved another inch.

"Legend, Andrew. *Legend.* Legend has it that the Temple of Aja is impregnable. For some reason, my memory only carried that as far as the elusive entrance. Only now did I remember the rest."

"And... what is the rest, sir?"

Brannigan shifted his weight carefully, gold coins tinkling at his feet. "This temple was built by King Olemode hundreds of years ago as a gift to his new wife Ejiro, and by proxy to Aja herself. Local lore tells that Ejiro enjoyed puzzles, and King Olemode–a very cruel man–took her love of puzzles in mind quite literally when he built this temple." Brannigan shook his head. "Wings of Icarus, how could I have been so stupid?"

"Puzzles, sir?"

"Puzzles, Andrew my boy. The Eye of Aja won't simply be laid out for the taking. It will be terribly more complicated than that."

Squatting, Brannigan began clearing coins and pearl necklaces from the floor at his feet, one piece of treasure at a time. When Andrew stooped to follow suit, Brannigan stopped him.

"Just wait, my boy. Let me see what lies beneath."

When the last coin was lifted, Brannigan beheld the stone floor of the dais.

Intricate tiles were visible, cut from a coarse brown

stone and interlocking. On the face of each was a glyph unlike any Brannigan had ever before seen. The Professor ran one hand across the rough surface slowly.

"Just as I feared," he said. "Warnings and directions. These tiles aren't tiles at all." Carefully, he put pressure on the surface at the seam of two 'tiles.' They moved slightly.

"What are they, Professor?"

"Triggers of sorts, Andrew." From his belt, Brannigan pulled his trusty Bowie knife and nosed the edge into the crack between two tiles and slid it inside. "You see, my boy, if this were a tile, I would not be able to do this." The blade was gone, disappeared in the floor to the hilt of the knife.

"What is that, Professor? These tiles..."

"They go straight down." Brannigan pulled the knife out. "At least eight inches or so. Huge pressure sensitive triggers."

"If you were to–" Andrew shifted his weight and, on tenuous footing, lost his balance. Arms pinwheeling, he fell. Brannigan was kneeling and rose, but somehow not in time to catch the young adventurer. Some reflexes!

Andrew fell, the flat of one palm slapping against the floor trigger Brannigan had just unearthed.

Nothing happened. At first.

Then the trigger began sinking.

The ground shifted beneath our adventurers feet, portions of the dais rising as others began sinking. Brannigan grabbed Caine's arm to steady the young man.

"Hold tight, my boy!"

"I'm sorry, Professor! I–"

"It was inevitable that one of us would trip something, Andrew. Fear not!"

Waves of coins rolled off piles of treasures at the edges of the dais as the tiles around the outside rose like walls. In the center–where our adventurers stood–the tiles dropped. Soon, they were immersed in a slowly sinking pit, coins tumbling down at them like golden rain.

Finally, the sinking floor beneath them stopped.

Jagged floor tiles could be seen rising above them like tiny steps now unearthed from the treasures. Conceivably, they could climb straight out. If the steps were *steps*, rather than more triggers. Hands on his hips and knee-deep in treasure, Brannigan realized what was going on.

"I'd say we're in a spot of trouble, my boy."

"What is it, Professor?"

"You see, we're standing on one great puzzle box. And with every step, the floor will change, and I've no doubt that a few of these triggers do more than simply make the floor raise or lower."

"What makes you say that, sir?"

Brannigan gave his best smile. "Because even now I can see the king cobra that was released on our first misstep."

Coiled a few feet from Brannigan was indeed a king cobra, head raised and hood opened menacingly. Two golden eyes turned and locked on Brannigan.

"Now what, sir?" Andrew asked.

"I don't know, Andrew. I just don't know. We've found ourselves in an unenviable position."

Outside, the first charges of dynamite were detonated with a terrible roar.

"Pistols, Ms. Halifax?"

Liliana was angry, an emotion only exacerbated by the fact that the barrel-chested security guard facing her took her anger to be hysteria.

"Yes, Mr. Gardner, I said *pistols.*"

"But I didn't see any gentlemen on the premises. Perhaps what you need to do is calm down–"

She waved a stern index finger at him like a truncheon. "Don't you say that to me *one more time*, Mr. Gardner. Yes, I said pistols. Men with *pistols.* I'm not being hysterical, nor am I hallucinating as you apparently think young women are wont to do. I am in full control of my faculties, I assure you."

The big man twisted up his face in consternation. Like most men she'd encountered since transferring to Branford University, Mr. Gardner seemed unprepared for a young lady to talk back to him rather than fold beneath his stern direction. "But Miss," he said with a frustrated sigh, "there are simply no men here, armed or otherwise. As you can see–"

"My name is *Dr. Halifax*, Mr. Gardner, and I would

appreciate it if you respected my degrees as you are so willing to do for the men of this Institute." Rare was it for Liliana Halifax to demand such formality–a habit she generally found rude and terribly arrogant–but Mr. Gardner was making her more and more *angry*. "Let me speak with your supervisor."

Mr. Elliot Gardner sighed, a noise that seemed to be pushing Dr. Halifax slowly towards insanity, and agreed. "Yes, *Doctor*." He turned and shuffled to the security desk at the far wall, his shoulders slumped.

She'd gone through too much in the past few hours to be defeated by a stubborn security guard. She would report this incident and get to the bottom of it.

After using the kitchenette's old refrigerator as a safe haven to escape the treacherous Mr. Smith (not to be tried at home, dear readers!), Dr. Halifax had waited until she could no longer bear the cold before tentatively opening the old door and crawling out.

The quaint kitchenette showed the tell-tale signs of a temper tantrum–angry damage incurred at the hands of Smith, she supposed–but thankfully no strange men with pistols. Halifax had left the kitchenette and wound through the hallways carefully, finding Ms. Peters' reception desk empty. A note reading "*Getting dinner, back soon!*" sat on the blotter.

Taking the stairs down two at a time, Dr. Halifax had rushed to the main security desk. On the ground floor, she'd found Mr. Gardner manning the circular desk at the Institute's front door. He was snoring.

Now here she was, waiting for his supervisor, whoever that was. *I've argued with him long enough,* she thought. Now she could argue with someone else. Why was this Mr. Gardner so unwilling to believe her? So unwilling to contact the police or even file a report? She touched the black disc tucked beneath her arm to make sure it was still there and hadn't been a figment of her imagination. *Still there,* she thought. *I'm not crazy.*

"Dr. Halifax?"

She turned to see Wanda Bullington smiling at her. Mrs. Bullington, assistant to the mysterious Quincy Max himself, was a slight woman in her sixties. She wore thick-framed glasses and had a kind face, complimented rather strangely by black hair cut in a severe bob.

"Mrs. Bullington," Dr. Halifax said, rather breathless from surprise. "What are you doing here?"

"I'm coming to check on you, dear. Are you all right?"

How could she know already? Dr. Halifax thought. "Well, yes, ma'am. I'm fine. Perhaps a little... a little bothered, but all right."

Mrs. Bullington turned and said something to Gardner, making the security guard blush and nod his head dumbly.

"Please, my dear, follow me."

The small woman led Dr. Halifax to a private elevator recessed in a corner of the library. Mrs. Bullington opened the gate with a golden key she removed from her pocket and pulled it shut behind Dr. Halifax. There was only one button on the panel. It said *Q*.

"Going up," Mrs. Bullington said with a smile.

The elevator cage groaned to life and began to rise, carrying the two silent women up to the Institute's top floor.

When the doors opened on the top floor, Dr. Halifax's breath caught in her throat.

The top floor was one large room, floor to ceiling

56

windows covered each wall, overlooking the late autumn landscape of Branford University. Scattered around the space were glass cases displaying an array of artifacts unlike any she'd seen before in a single place.

Gilded and bejeweled skulls, ancient Sanskrit maps, scrolls from the Dark Ages pressed between thick sheets of glass, and a half-dozen other relics that Dr. Halifax herself could not even identify.

"Dr. Halifax?" a wizened voice called from the far end of the great room.

Mrs. Bullington led her from the elevator and across the space, Halifax's eyes lingering over each glass case.

"Dr. Halifax," Mrs. Bullington introduced as the two women arrived at a huge wooden desk. "This is Dr. Quincy Max."

From behind the desk, a thin old man stood, one shaking hand clutching the curved head of a cane. His body seemed gaunt and weak, but his smile was bright and alive, buried deep in a huge white beard that hung to his mid-chest. He extended one hand. "Hello, my dear, hello! My name is Quincy Max. It's a genuine pleasure to meet you, Dr. Halifax."

Liliana Halifax shook the old man's hand gently, smiling for the first time since receiving the strange package. Her anger finally abated—if only slightly—as she said, "It is an honor to meet you, sir."

"Have a seat, have a seat," he said, gesturing to a chair before his desk. Beside her, Mrs. Bullington slipped away, leaving Dr. Halifax alone with the old man.

"Doctor please forgive me for not welcoming you to our Institute here at Branford University before now. And to welcome you after such an evening as you've had, oh dear, I'm terribly sorry."

"Not at all, Doctor, please."

"I have to admit, while this isn't the first time we've had men wander the halls of our Institute with pistols in their hands and malice in their hearts, it certainly is the first time since I was a much younger man. Things were different when I was just a faculty member. I had a habit of getting myself into some trouble, let me tell you."

Halifax smiled. "I'm sorry to hear that, sir."

"No, no, my dear. The only regret I have is that I'm not a young man myself, anymore. Oh, the times I've spent running through jungle brush, chased by poisoned arrows and hot-leaded bullets. Those were the days."

Dr. Halifax had no idea what to say. Their field was *academics*, wasn't it?

"Anyway, I digress. First, I'd like to apologize for Mr. Gardner and the lax impression you must have gotten from our security. I assure you, it will not happen again. Wanda is tending to our security troubles even as we speak."

"No need to apologize, sir. Really."

He smiled again, a rather infectious smile. "Well, I expect you'd like an explanation," the old man said as he rose to his feet. When Dr. Halifax went to follow, he motioned for her to keep her seat.

From a cabinet beside his desk, Max pulled a scroll, brown and faded with age. Unsteadily, he reached out and handed it to her. She rested the onyx disc in her lap and unrolled the scroll.

"What is this, sir?" Halifax said, her eyes moving over the script.

"A piece of paper that will change your life, I believe," he said with a grin. "It is a sort of inventory of *Orisha,*

58

manifestations of God in a specific region of Africa."

Halifax's eyes began recognizing certain symbols. "Yoruba," she said softly.

"Yes, indeed." She looked up to see a twinkle in the old man's eyes. "I knew I'd chosen you well."

She frowned. "Sir?"

"Your work on international mythology and the unifying theories of which you've written," he said. "I have read them and found them quite illuminating."

She opened her mouth to speak but only managed to sputter. "Those were published under a pseudonym," she said. "Those... they–"

"Please forgive me, Doctor. I know you tried to distance yourself from them as much as possible, but they were too brilliant to go unnoticed."

"I'm sorry?"

"Not long ago, a dear friend of mine named Ellis Spooner put a controversial scientific journal on my desk and pointed at an essay written by Iliana di Sogno–a pseudonym, of course. It advocated certain mythologies and religious entities across religions, but lingered on the Yoruba in particular. This Iliana di Sogno hypothesized that the Yoruba people, though found in Africa, had traveled from somewhere else in the world, and had much farther reaches of religious influence. It was denied by most, but some of us found it quite interesting."

"How did you–"

Quincy waved her off. "It's not important how we found you, really. But I think you are correct in your theories, and I think the scroll in your hands will confirm it."

She examined it more closely. Yoruba in origin,

somehow it was touched with an international flavor. In the script she translated, Dr. Halifax recognized references to gods and monsters from disparate lands, ranging from Scandinavian folklore to Melanesian mythology. And yet, all of it seemed filtered through a Yoruba lens.

"This is..." She trailed off, shaking her head. "Impossible."

Quincy laughed. "I assure you, Dr. Halifax, it's real. That was sent to me from Brick Brannigan."

Dr. Halifax looked up. "Dr. Brannigan?"

Quincy nodded. "The same man who was meant to sign for the package that got you into so much trouble today."

Halifax lowered the scroll and moved it aside for a moment. In her lap lay the onyx disc that had nearly gotten her killed. She looked up to see Quincy's sparkling blue eyes resting on the disc as well.

"May I?" he asked.

"Of course."

He took the disc gingerly, his knotted old hands moving over it with a delicate touch that bordered on reverence. "It is true," he said in a whisper. "At last, Ellis, you did it."

"What is it, sir?"

He looked up. "My friend Professor Spooner has been searching for this for years. I believe this to be the Cipher of Dumuzid. He finally found it, and in the jungles of Africa, just as he suspected."

Dr. Halifax frowned. "Dumuzid, sir? But Dumuzid is... Sumerian."

Quincy smiled. "What was it you wrote, Doctor? 'It is

my informed opinion that the link between Yoruba and Sumer, while unlikely, cannot be discounted without firm proof.' You found linguistic parallels, did you not?"

"I did, but I never thought–"

"That you could truly be correct?" Quincy couldn't help but smile once again. "It seems that perhaps you were correct, after all. And it is only the tip of the iceberg. These connections bridge more religions than that of Sumer and Yoruba, as the scroll proves. Now you have your proof. Soon, we will have more."

"Why?"

"That Cipher, if I am correct, can be used to decode the unknown glyphs on the scroll in your hands, glyphs that I believe directly link Sumer and Yoruba. I've been searching for the Cipher of Dumuzid for many, many years."

"And now you have it."

"Yes. It seems Ellis has found it. Remarkable, indeed!"

"Doctors Spooner and Brannigan, sir. Pardon me for asking, but who are they really?"

Quincy looked up. "What do you mean?"

"Well, from what I've heard, they seem more globetrotters than Professors of Archaeology."

The old man smiled. "That they are, my dear."

"I'm sorry, Doctor, but what does this have to do with–"

"Men with pistols? Deities of Yoruba and Sumer? Ancient scrolls and codes? It all has to do with something originally called the Axé of Ogoun."

"Sir?"

"The Axé of Ogoun was formed deep in the jungles of Nigeria long ago, a group of men and women exiled from the Yoruba culture after deifying the most dangerous and violent aspects of the Orisha Ogoun."

"Ogoun," Halifax said, "The Yoruba deity of iron and war?"

"Yes, indeed!" Quincy laughed, delighted. "Well, in the years after being exiled from Yoruba, the Axé of Ogoun evolved, eventually wandering from the true teachings of Yoruba and becoming something wholly different. Wholly... *evil.* Today, their reach is global, and they grow with each passing day. Over the years, they united faiths and folklore from around the world, crushing them together along with their own terrible ideologies to make something entirely unique–and entirely terrible. Today they are known as the Cabal of Angelus Mortis."

Halifax shook her head. "This is... so much. So strange," she said softly. "All this... what does this have to do with me? What does it have to do with this scroll in my hands and the Cipher you hold?"

Quincy smiled sadly. "Your theories led me to bring you onto the staff here at the Institute, but you were not truly involved until you signed for a package today. Ellis Spooner has been searching for the Cipher for many years, and Brick Brannigan unsuccessfully searching for the relics associated with it. Using the Cipher, we hope to prevent the Cabal from bringing together a host of these relics and artifacts to consolidate their power. In doing so they hope to unite behind a common goal: destroying the world."

Liliana's mouth fell open. "Destroying the world?" she said. Even she could not stop the next word that escaped her lips. "Seriously?"

Quincy laughed, loud and without restraint. He leaned back in his chair and really let go. Dr. Halifax looked at him, feeling nothing but lost. A few hours ago, her biggest concern was dusting her desk. Now this?

After a long moment given to collect himself, Quincy said, "It's true, my dear. However strange or unlikely it seems, it is unfortunately true. We do live in a day and age when the destruction of the world has become a legitimate life goal. Can you believe it?"

"And so this Cabal hopes to bring together artifacts from around the world? What will that accomplish?"

"When brought together, these relics will create a force unlike anything previously known to this earth. I believe this power is why each religion has their own precious icons and artifacts, and why they are spread so far apart on the globe."

"Because if brought together, they will create a power capable of..."

The old man nodded. "Destroying the world."

"And what do the Cipher of Dumuzid and the scroll have to do with it again?"

"I believe they will help us locate these artifacts before the Cabal."

"And why exactly is an Institute at a University in rural Illinois doing this? Why is it not a global priority? Armies and presidents and kings should be losing sleep over this."

"Have you ever tried to convince global leaders that the world is being threatened by an age-old secret Cabal bent on harnessing the power of religious relics in order to destroy all civilization and perhaps the very fabric of the universe as we know it?"

"No."

"Well, it is more difficult than it sounds," he said frowning.

"I can imagine," she nodded. "And now what?"

Quincy lay the Cipher on his desk and leaned back. "Now the true hunt begins. Even before applying the Cipher to the scroll, Brick was in search of a relic he believed he'd gotten a line on: the Eye of Aja."

"The Eye of Aja? But that's only a legend!" Dr. Halifax exclaimed.

Quincy smiled. "Oh, no, Doctor. It is indeed real, and if Brick is correct, it lays at the heart of it all, where this terrible journey began so many years ago when the Yoruba exiled the Axé of Ogoun: in the heart of the Niger delta."

"And this... Brick Brannigan, sir?"

"He is doing his best to liberate the Eye of Aja from the jungles of Nigeria even as we speak. Before it falls into the hands of the Cabal." His face paled and his voice grew serious. "It is only the first step in a line of many, but much is at stake. Not just the life of Brick Brannigan, Dr. Halifax, but the very fate of the world!"

Dr. Halifax thought of her New Year's resolution to take more risks. In the blink of an eye, her boring life had been turned upside down. She suddenly found herself up to her eyeballs in risk, even danger. All at once, the world was at stake, and she was truly in the thick of it. Trouble had arrived–and in spades!

Despite her better judgement, she couldn't help but feel excitement at the realization.

Before she could stop herself, she was asking, "How can I help?"

CHAPTER 11: In Which Our Heroes Use the Terrible Curses of Aja as a Fearsome Weapon!

Brannigan had sunk deep in a pit, the trigger-like floor tiles beneath his feet shifting with each dreadful step. In addition to the king cobra he'd unleashed (who had proceeded to lose interest in our adventurers and focus his primal attentions on the multitude of rodents that scurried in the temple's dark corners) Brannigan had set free a host of angry bats, a cache of poisonous spiders, and a legion of bright red fire ants. Trap doors and tiny openings seemed to reveal themselves with each of his missplaced steps. The great hero had finally decided to stop moving, his weight awkwardly balanced on a few tiles at the bottom of the newly-formed pit.

As the floor of the great dais had sunken and the beasts were unleashed, Brannigan had urged Caine to continue climbing. Now, with the floor in the center of the dais over twenty feet below the floor at the outer rim, Brannigan seemed to have been swallowed by the strange puzzle floor.

Caine–light and acrobatic in comparison to Brannigan– was now very near the edge, hands gripping the step-like floor tiles as he reached for the very edge of the dais to pull himself up to the level where they'd once begun their endeavor.

"Almost there, Andrew!" Brannigan shouted. Sweat was pouring off his filthy face, and for the first time that day, he was beginning to worry.

The first blast of dynamite had done little more than shake loose dust and loose tiles from the temple's high ceiling. The second had sent long narrow cracks running along the room's southeast wall. The third had opened the narrow cracks, transforming them into great dark fissures. Even now, the muffled sound of shouts could be heard from beyond, and the faintest hint of sunlight threatened to creep inside the hallowed chamber.

"What am I climbing for, Professor?" young Caine asked. With a heave, he pulled himself upwards, lifting himself with shaking arms. Beneath his kicking feet, Brannigan watched with baited breath as tiles sank and shifted. A moment later, the grating of stone on stone sounded in the chamber, heralding trouble.

A new trap door had opened at the far end of Brannigan's pit and a pair of yellow eyes peered out at him from the darkness.

"Professor?"

"I don't know what it is, Andrew, and I'd prefer not to know!"

"What now, sir?"

"Hm?"

"What now?"

Brannigan looked up. Young Caine was standing on the edge of the pit, beads of sweat pouring from his face as he struggled to catch his breath.

"Good show, Andrew! You've reached the top. Well done, lad!"

"Thanks, Professor."

"Now, there should be some safety catch... some kind of device to deactivate this damnable puzzle floor!" He shifted his weight, the muscles in his legs beginning to burn from the exertion of not moving. As it was, he stood precariously balanced, unable to move his feet and fearful to move anything else lest he lose his balance and fall.

"What will it look like, Professor?"

Brannigan scratched his mustache. "Well," he said. "A... um. How about..." He thought some more. A trigger or hidden button? Perhaps it would be masked as a statuesque bust of Aja herself?

"Sir?"

"Well, Andrew, I must admit, my dear boy: I've not the foggiest idea what the safety release looks like. To make matters worse, there is a temple I discovered in Burma that had no safety catch at all! So that is it's own problem." He shook his head.

"Here's what I want you to do, Andrew. Go–"

Another package of dynamite exploded, throwing Brannigan to his knees as huge stone bricks fell from the ceiling as the great fissure in the southeast wall opened, unleashing a bright beam of sunlight from the jungle outside.

As Brannigan fell, a slit opened a few inches away, releasing two brightly colored tree frogs unlike anything Brannigan had ever before beheld. They leapt past him without giving the great man a second glance.

"Professor!"

Brannigan lifted his head to see a flurry of Black Fang's Legion of Madmen pour through the fissure, rifles and pistols at the ready.

Leading the charge was Von Faust, a maniacal grin on

his face and Luger in hand. Standing at the back of the group on the edge of the detonation site, Black Fang himself looked over the unfolding scene with a smirk, his hand resting on the gilded hilt of his scimitar.

"Run, Andrew!" Brannigan shouted as he clambered up from the pit. "Fall back, my boy. Towards the entrance!"

Realizing that their only chance lay in luck and ingenuity, Brannigan took off, his great hands and feet slamming against as many different trigger tiles as he could reach.

He heard a symphony of hidden doorways rising, trapdoors falling open, and the floor of the puzzle dais rising and falling beneath him like a living creature. Moments later, a maelstrom was unleashed.

Above him, amidst a group of Fang's Madmen, a wild-eyed tiger stepped free of its former confines, hunger burning in its eyes. The zealots after Brannigan's head turned their attentions to the temple's beasts as the creatures poured from hidden passages everywhere.

Brannigan did not pause as the king cobra lashed out, sinking its venomous fangs into a young soldier's calf; he did not blink as he saw a tall bearded fellow topple at the wretchedly poisonous attack of the tree frogs; he did not dare breathe as he leapt over a screaming man swallowed beneath an army of terrible fire ants.

Young Andrew Caine led the way, feet slamming against trick floor tiles as he ran, unleashing further creatures upon the unsuspecting Legion of Madmen, but little did they care–they *were* mad, after all!

Panthers and lions entered the fray. Even the crocodile who had followed our adventurers into the temple had his taste of a Madman.

"Quite a cornucopia of predators, my boy!" Brannigan shouted as they approached the doorway. Behind him, he could hear shouting mixed with the roar of predatory beasts and the sharp bite of gunfire.

Ten feet from the door that led back towards the flooded antechamber, Brannigan lurched to a stop. To his right, he saw something strange hidden in the recesses of the chamber.

"A door?" he said. "To where? That can't be correct."

"What is it, Professor?"

Brannigan pointed. "There, my boy. Do you see it? Buried in the darkest corner."

Young Caine squinted into the darkness, leaning forward over the moat.

"I don't see anything, sir."

Brannigan extended his pointing arm further. "There, lad. Just there beneath–"

The *whiz* of a bullet interrupted him as it cut through the flesh of his forearm, a fine mist of blood filling the air between our two adventurers. Brannigan pulled his arm back with a hiss.

He turned to see Von Faust running towards him, maniacal grin still in place, his Luger extended out in front of him, smoke curling from the barrel.

Brannigan felt, almost in slow motion, his foot depress one final trick floor tile, and fast as he was, he was not fast enough to stop it. Ignoring Von Faust for the moment–as only the incredibly poised Brick Brannigan could–the Professor watched and waited the long few seconds for the fruits of the trap to be released.

Nothing happened. Brannigan believed them safe until he saw a soldier–busy battling with a ferocious spotted leopard–drop his rifle and grab his throat as he collapsed. In a moment, he was dead.

"Poisonous gas," Brannigan whispered. "It seems I've saved the worst for last. Damn the builders of this deathtrap, leaving the deadliest curse so close to the exit." He turned to young Caine. "Cover your mouth, my boy!"

"Don't move, Brannigan!" Von Faust shouted, still closing on our adventurers. "You're mine now, *du missgeburt!*"

Brannigan raised a shirtsleeve to cover his mouth and nose. "I don't speak German, you fearsome dunce! I keep meaning to learn, honestly, but–oh nevermind! At the moment, you are the least of my worries!"

Von Faust's face twisted in consternation, his one good eye glaring suspiciously. He cast a glance over his shoulder to see soldiers fleeing for their lives. In the spotty light of the chamber, our adventurers and Von Faust alike could now see long wisps of a greenish gas hissing from slits in the temple floor. Curling like long tails into the air, the poison gas had begun to exact its terrible toll on all who remained.

From his position at the mouth of the detonation site, Black Fang understood all too well what was happening and what it meant. He took a step back, turning to an assistant. Brannigan could see Fang speak, but the words were lost over the great distance. Black Fang's assistant disappeared momentarily before returning, dragging a wooden crate behind him.

It was a fresh case of dynamite!

"He means to seal us inside," Brannigan said. "Madness! That bastard Fang understands that he cannot enter, so he will seal the crack and let us die of the poison here inside."

Von Faust's mouth fell open. "Not me, no Herr Delacroix!" He turned, his Luger hanging limply at his side. "No! Please wait!"

Von Faust took off across the room, stepping over countless dead men before sputtering to a halt near the center of the room. The fumes were too much. His face covered with a handkerchief and eyes burning, he backpedaled away from the plumes of poisonous gas, Black Fang shaking his head sadly to lose so many of his loyal Madmen.

Von Faust returned to Brannigan, Luger holstered, just as the fresh bundle of dynamite detonated in the newly formed entrance cut from the temple wall. The thick stone wall collapsed in a storm of brick and earth, sealing the Temple of Aja and the few who still remained inside alive. Above them, huge stones began falling from the already weakened structure in a deadly rainfall. They were trapped.

"No further time to waste, Andrew!" Brannigan shouted. "I believe the Temple of Aja is not long for this world. Black Fang knows it's easier to dig through rubble for priceless artifacts than to battle us for them!" He turned and dashed across the dais, his sleeve still pressed firmly to his nose and mouth, and began tugging at the door from which they'd first entered.

He pushed and pulled with all his incredible might, even with young Caine at his side, but the door did not budge. In another moment, Von Faust offered strained assistance, the three men pushing with all their strength as they fought for their lives.

The door did not open.

"Is all lost, Professor?" Caine asked.

"It is not ever lost, my boy," Brannigan said solemnly.

"You are a fool Brannigan! It was you who brought this death upon us this day! It is all your fault!" Von Faust raised his Luger menacingly.

Brannigan swatted the German's arm away. "Not now, you dunderhead! We've lives to save. Our own!"

Pushing Von Faust out of his way, Brannigan led young Caine into the dark corner of the chamber, all the while praying that his eyes had not been playing tricks on him.

They hadn't.

Secreted in the corner beneath the thickest blanket of shadows was a door, small and simple, becoming nearly invisible against the like-colored stone of the wall.

But there was no knob or lock release. It was as if the door was no door at all.

"There must be a way," Brannigan muttered. "There must be!"

Behind them, even the most terrible of the predators released by the puzzle floor were dying at the hands of the poisonous gas that slowly filled the room. Soon, our gang of three were the only things left in the room alive–and barely at that! Other than Brannigan's frantic searchings for a way through the door, the only other sound in the room was the ominous *hisssssssssss* of the gas.

"Break it down, Brannigan!" Von Faust coughed. "Just break it! The strength is leaving my body!"

Much as Brannigan would have liked to decry the ravings of Von Faust, he couldn't, for even Brannigan's superhuman strength seemed to be waning.

"If I cannot use my strength," Brannigan muttered, "I will use my wits."

He ran his hand across the inset frame of the door, searching for a button or hidden release. There was nothing. He then knelt and felt along the floor, seeing as how much the creators of the temple seemed to like trick floor tiles. Again, there was nothing.

Beside him, young Caine began coughing terribly, his thin frame leaning against the wall, nigh lifelessly!

"Hold on, Andrew. Hold on, my boy!"

Finally, Brannigan ran his hand across the face of the door itself. He knew not what else he could do. Near the floor and off to the side was a flat button disguised as nothing more than a pebble. Brannigan pushed it desperately.

The door slid open and the three men tumbled through. In a moment, the door shut behind them.

Caine lay on the floor, face pale and panting. Brannigan knelt at his side.

"It's all right now, my boy. Breathe normally! Breathe normally."

Von Faust stood over them, an evil grin spreading across his face once more. For even though Brannigan had just saved his life, dear reader, we overlook the fact that Von Faust is mad, madder even, perhaps, than Black Fang Delacroix himself. Rather than be grateful, his terrible cause was undeterred.

He raised his Luger at the back of Brannigan's skull.

Young Caine opened his eyes slowly, the color of his face beginning to return to normal. "Professor," he gasped. "Professor!"

Brannigan turned, and with lightning quick hands he snatched the Luger from Von Faust before the Nazi could even fathom what was happening. The one-eyed monster grimaced.

"You bastard, Brannigan!"

"Shut up, Von Faust! I've not the time nor the patience to listen to or worry about the words of a chucklehead like you. I've saved our lives once, and I will do so again in freeing us of this terrible tomb. But if you raise a finger to me once more, I will leave you here to die a slow death!"

Von Faust sputtered over a handful of retorts, but the primal instinct to survive was enough to keep his yap shut.

"Sputter on, you dolt, and in the meantime I will be searching for our exit!" Brannigan said, heaving young Caine to his feet.

Turning from Von Faust, our two adventurers followed the secret corridor down, down deep into the depths of the Temple of Aja and whatever the darkness below had waiting for them.

CHAPTER 12: In Which Our Heroes Find Mortal Danger at the Hands of a Brilliantly Terrible Machine

In the darkness of the corridor, none of the unlikely trio spoke. Brannigan led the way, walking slowly down the descending tunnel. Behind him, young Caine followed the sound of the great Professor's footsteps. At the back was Von Faust, sniveling with each step.

"Where are you leading us, Brannigan?"

"This tunnel leads down, Von Faust. Considering we've encountered neither a fork in the road nor a door, I am going the only way possible. Have you a unique suggestion?"

Von Faust had nothing to add but complaints. Brannigan ignored him.

The tunnel curved to the right before finally bottoming out before an open doorway. The narrow corridor opened into a huge room somehow lit with mirrors angling bright sunshine from outside. The ceiling was very low–just high enough to accommodate Brannigan's great stature–but the room itself seemed to continue endlessly into the darkness. The sunshine, so unnatural in the dark room, shot across the open space in narrow columns, leaving only bright slashes of light, giving the room a strange zebra skin-like quality.

"What is this place, Professor?"

Brannigan shook his head. "I don't know, Andrew. Although with that last curve of the tunnel, we seem to be directly beneath the main room of the temple."

"If there is sunlight..." Von Faust began. He dashed across the space to the nearest mirror that angled light into the room. Clambering at the wall like a trapped cat, Von Faust quickly realized the light came from holes no larger than the heel of a shoe.

"Blast," the Nazi sighed. "Still trapped."

"Don't be too certain, Von Faust," Brannigan said. "There is always a second entrance. The question you should be asking is: what is this chamber's purpose?"

The Professor began walking deeper into the room, soon leaving young Caine and Von Faust behind him in the shadows. The room was cool and smelled like wet soil, the only sound the scrape of Brannigan's boots on the packed dirt floor. He walked deeper and deeper, his curiosity pulling him into the shadows.

At a certain point, he realized he was holding his breath, and finally reaching the back wall of the great chamber, Brannigan released his breath very slowly.

Before him lay an iron-banded wooden chest, surrounded in a halo of bright reflected sunlight.

"What is that?" Von Faust whispered from behind him.

"Professor...?" Caine asked.

Brannigan shook his head. "I've no idea," he said. "I know what I wish it to be, but I do not know what it is, in truth."

Kneeling, our hero ran a hand along the rusted iron that trimmed the chest. "It is not like anything else here in the Temple of Aja. It is as anachronistic as the arches adorning the facade outside." He stroked his mustache and ran a hand through his damp hair.

"Who put it here?" Caine asked.

"I don't know, my boy." Brannigan snapped back the metal latch, ever so carefully. "The Yoruba people were reclusive, but this chest and the arches outside lead me to believe that builders of this temple were not totally isolated..."

Von Faust spoke up, his voice wavering slightly. "Brannigan, I..." He trailed off.

Brick Brannigan, smart enough to know the presages of honesty when he heard them, turned to peer over his shoulder at Von Faust. "What is it, Captain?"

Von Faust wiped a copious amount of sweat from his face with his sleeve. "When we were researching the temple, we found reason to believe that the Yoruba people knew of the Cabal..."

Brannigan sneered. "You speak of the Cabal like some distant fiction when you yourself are in their employ!" His voice rose angrily. "And your boss, Fang!"

Von Faust shook his head. "Unlike myself, Herr Delacroix has not sworn allegiance to the Cabal, sir. He is a mere contractor. He is no true believer."

To Brannigan, it was nothing more than semantics. Black Fang Delacroix may not have been a *true* member of the Cabal, but he still pursued the holy relics with the same nefarious purpose. "What was the point, sir?"

"Only that we found records that the Yoruba may have employed outside help in creating the elaborate machines that protect this temple. Herr Delacroix and the Master wanted us to be ready."

It was of Brannigan's opinion that Von Faust could not

be ready for a rainstorm had he carried an umbrella in each hand. Regardless, he would be foolish not to heed some caution. And so, from his belt he pulled Von Faust's Luger and pulled back the hammer with his thumb.

With a grunt, he lifted the lid of the chest.

Inside, a rope pulled taut as the lid opened, snapping free like a booby trap's trigger. Brannigan flinched, but nothing happened.

Von Faust groaned. "I believe that was an explosive, no? Perhaps that was the trap. Do you believe the charge has expired due to age?"

Brannigan shook his head. "This was no bomb." He stood and took a step back.

Inside the chest was a meaningless pile of machinery, cogs and wheels, spokes and ratchets, bolts and joints, all haphazardly lying one atop the other. A senseless mess of steel, iron, grease, and wasted ingenuity, Brannigan thought.

"Not the Eye of Aja," he sighed. "But what is it?"

"Scrap," Von Faust muttered. "A dead end. Black Fang's worst fear was true: we have been beaten to this relic by someone else. The Eye is gone."

Brannigan shook his head. "No," he said. "I believe it is here. Perhaps it is even–"

A *screeeech* of metal interrupted him mid-sentence. Unconsciously, he took a step back.

"Professor, sir?" Caine said softly. "Did you hear that?"

"Aye, my boy. It was perhaps–"

SCRAAAASSHHH. Another frightful sound escaped the chest, a scream of metal on metal. Before anyone could speak, a coil of greased chain shifted, growing tight, like a snake waking from sleep.

"Step back," Brannigan said.

"What is that?" Von Faust gasped. "No, no! It's a machine ghost! A demon!"

"Silence your ravings, Heinrich, and step back!"

All together, the unlikely gang withdrew a few paces further as the cogs began turning.

Click... click... click click... click click... click click... click click click... like the ticking of a clock warily coming back to life after years of disrepair and maltreatment. Finally, something caught.

Clickclickclickclickclickclickclick.... The machine's heart kickstarted.

Disparate pieces united, screws twisted their ways into threaded holes, bolts tightened. The flat array of junk began to take shape.

"Professor..."

"Stand tall, lad."

Slowly, terribly slowly, a shape began to rise from the chest, pushed on by the steady whirring of some machinery, the horrible *clickclickclickclick* ever present.

A hand slapped down on the edge of the chest, straining to lift something free from the confines of the wood and iron. The fingers, not knit together from flesh and bone, were instead forged in gleaming steel and animated by spinning cogs and ratcheting wheels.

A second hand followed the first.

Finally, with a mechanical *zzzzzzz* of exertion, a head rose from the wooden box. A head, giving way to a neck and chest. A Clockwork Man ascended.

"Fall back," Von Faust pleaded. "We must retreat, Herr Brannigan."

"Fall back where, you cretin? We are trapped beneath a collapsing temple. At any moment, this very chamber could be crushed..."

"Then fire your pistol! If you won't fire, then let me!"

"We must conserve ammunition!"

The Clockwork Man stepped free of the chest, metal feet digging into the earthen floor. One step, uneasy at first, then a second. With each step, the machine grew steadier on its manmade feet.

"Shoot, Brannigan!"

Brannigan raised the pistol, but his trigger finger extended straight out against the guard. "It's a machine, Von Faust, not a man!"

"Kill it!" Von Faust screeched.

Ignoring him, Brannigan said, "Can... can you understand me? Are you a man or a machine?"

The Clockwork Man did not respond–not entirely surprising–taking instead another step towards them. A tight chain began to wind as the machine's arm rose and its humanlike robo-fist opened.

"Professor..." Caine whispered, his slight body racked with terror. "What... what does it want?"

"Be strong, my boy. All is not lost." Brannigan's eyes moved over the machine, taking in each gear and crankshaft, probing for a single point of weakness.

"Fool, Brannigan, you will be the death of us!"

"Silence, Von Faust!"

Unable to contain himself any longer, Von Faust leapt at Brannigan, his fascist hands clambering for the Luger.

80

In the struggle, Brannigan raised the pistol, extended his arms from Von Faust's manic grip. Young Caine took a step towards the grappling men, swinging a fist at Von Faust, the punch glancing off the Nazi officer's cheek.

Von Faust's hands closed over Brannigan's, and in the tight space of the subterranean chamber, the Luger discharged into the ceiling. The sound was incredibly loud, filling all three men's ears with a terrible ringing.

The Clockwork Man continued towards them, his pace measured but persistent.

With a frustrated groan, Brannigan twisted and heaved Von Faust up over his shoulder and face first onto the packed dirt floor. The evil Captain landed with a proverbial splat.

At the feet of the Clockwork Man.

"Get back, Von Faust, the mechanical beast is upon you!" Brannigan shouted.

Von Faust lifted his head in time for a metal hand to close over his throat. With a whirring of gears and clanking of minuscule engines, the Nazi was lifted from his feet as if he weighed nothing at all.

Feet kicking, he hung suspended, bald head against the ceiling.

"Let him be, Machine!" Brannigan shouted, raising the Luger as his finger finally tightened on the trigger. "The only man to do harm to mine villains is myself!"

Squeezing the trigger, Brannigan focused on what he'd decided was the machine's most obvious weak spot.

The bullet buried itself in a nest of servomechanisms in the Clockwork Man's knee. Machinery buckled and the knee gave way under the strain of Von Faust's added weight. The Machine Man tumbled to the ground with

Von Faust in tow.

Mechanical hand releasing the Nazi Captain's throat, the Clockwork Man turned his attention to Brannigan, lifting its skull with a menacing slowness that made the hair on the Professor's neck stand on end.

In place of eyes were two diamonds, pure white and perfectly cut. In the place of a mouth was a crosshatched iron grill, rusted and decrepit from its long stay inside the damp wooden chest. Once again, the Clockwork Man extended one open hand towards Brannigan.

"Get back, Von Faust!" Brannigan shouted. As the Nazi dragged himself free, Brannigan let loose with the Luger.

Shots rang out, one after another after another, 7.65 mm bullets pelting against the metal face and body of the machine, kicking off sparks and biting deeply into the mechanical body.

It did not slow the machine one iota.

Brannigan grabbed Von Faust's body and dragged him back, the Nazi officer struggling to take a complete breath. Dragging Von Faust, Brannigan said, "Andrew, check for an exit. There must be an exit! There must be!"

Pulling Von Faust well back from the Clockwork Man, Brannigan released him. Kneeling at his side, he said, "Captain, can you hear me?"

Von Faust nodded. "Unfortunately, you Yankee bastard."

Brannigan barked a laugh and looked up, seeing the strange machine had not given up. Unable to walk, it dragged itself towards them, its one hand remaining outstretched, fingers reaching to them.

Von Faust struggled into a sitting position, his single

82

eye wide with fear. "Brannigan, I cannot die down here. I cannot die beside *YOU!* A terrible shame if ever I could dream of one."

"Shut up, Von Faust," Brannigan said. "We're alive yet. And I intend to leave this chamber on my own two feet."

The *clickclickclick* had changed in frequency, ratcheting up to a frantic bumble-bee pace. Brannigan raised his head to see the machine struggling to right itself. Slowly, very slowly, it raised itself back to two feet.

"It's repaired itself," Von Faust said. "My God look at it! We are surely doomed, Brannigan!"

Professor Brick Brannigan opened his mouth to shout some retort, but no words came, his confidence faltering.

We may be in real trouble, he thought. *Truly.*

The Clockwork man began his slow walk towards them, diamond eyes glinting in the beams of sunlight.

CHAPTER 13: In Which Dr. Halifax Becomes a True Adventuress

Dr. Liliana Halifax was sitting on a red leather bench seat, white-gloved hands uneasily resting in her lap. Surrounding her was an army of bags, large and small and every size in between.

She crossed her legs. She uncrossed her legs. She straightened the red felt cloche on her head. She took the cloche off and tightened her hair in its bun. She returned the cloche.

Anxious was an understatement. Dr. Halifax was feeling an overwhelming sense of *fear*. What was she doing there again? What had compelled her to listen to Quincy Max? How had she found herself in his closest group of confidants, alongside rogue academics like Ellis Spooner and Hugo Brannigan? Did Max say his name was Brick? What kind of a name was Brick, again?

She stood, straightening her tweed jacket over her dress. "I'm leaving," she said aloud to the empty terminal. "I'm leaving."

Still, she did not move.

Somewhere in the distance, she heard the sound of a voice. She fiddled with her gloves, pulling them off her slender hands and wringing the leather tightly before slipping them back on. Finally, she returned to the bench seat.

She had already completed this routine a number of times, and until her pilot appeared, there was a great possibility it would continue.

Thankfully, her pilot *did* appear.

"Miss Halifax?" a suave voice ventured from over her shoulder.

She stood and turned, eyes beholding an average sized man with an oversized chin cleft. Beneath a pair of large reflective aviator sunglasses, he smiled broadly with perfect white teeth, the overhead lights of the private airport terminal reflecting off well-shaven cheeks. A tussle of dirty blonde hair perched rakishly atop his head.

Halifax blurted, "It's *Doctor* Halifax," before she could stop herself. After the encounter with the security guard, it was becoming a habit–a bad habit. "Oh," she said, smiling awkwardly. "Excuse me."

"No reason to beg pardon, madam," the man smiled and rested two fists on his hips. "If you are a doctor, your degree is well-earned." He smiled once more and removed his aviator sunglasses.

The rakish pilot had a thick English accent, Halifax noted. And remarkably lovely eyes.

"I would agree," Halifax said. She found herself smiling and extending a hand, hoping her red lipstick hadn't smudged in the time she'd had to fool with it. "And you are? Mister...?"

"Nero. Archibald Nero. A pleasure to meet you." He took her hand and raised it to his lips, kissing it delicately.

"Oh, that's not necessary, Mr. Nero," she said, suddenly feeling sheepish. She had to remember where she was and what she was doing, keeping the fact that she'd been feeling a loneliness since arriving at Branford University a non-issue. Still, it felt good having the attentions of a good-looking man.

"Not at all, Doctor, not at all." He slipped his glasses into the inside pocket of his wool-lined leather flight jacket. "Are these your bags?"

"Yes, Mr. Nero, these are my bags. Some are clothing, and some were sent along by Dr. Quincy Max himself."

Nero nodded. "I suspected," he said. "I fly exclusively for the University, although really I'm on Quincy's payroll. That old devil's treated me quite well." With nary a grunt, he single-handedly lifted the majority of her bags in his two hands and took off down the terminal to a door marked **TARMAC**, leaving a hatbox, attaché case, and leather shoulder bag behind for Dr. Halifax.

"Have you got that, Doctor?"

"Yes, Mr. Nero," she said. "I'm right behind you!"

The unlikely duo pushed through the double-doors leading out onto the tarmac. Night had fallen since Dr. Halifax had left the Institute, and the night sky was a beautiful dark cobalt blue, spotted with the most perfect menagerie of stars. She could not help look upward with wonder, something she'd done since she was a child and she hoped she would always do.

"Where are we going, Mr. Nero?"

"Uh, I had rather hoped Quincy had spoken to you, Doctor."

"Well, he did. Dr. Max and I spoke plenty, let me assure you–"

"Ah, all right."

"–but he did not go into much detail. I have to admit, Mr. Nero, I prefer to *know* the details rather than be forced to guess."

Nero laughed. "Well, Doctor, at this moment we're on our way out to my craft. Brand new, straight off the line Curtiss C-46 Commando–I call her Bell, short for *Belladonna*–where we'll board, get your menagerie of baggage strapped down, and we'll be on our way."

Struggling to keep up with Nero's long paces, Dr. Halifax said, "Uh, Mr. Nero, we are going to Africa, is that correct? It is my understanding that we'll be flying direct into a place called Rivers State? In Nigeria?"

Nero laughed again, a proud jubilant sound. "Indeed, Doctor. Although we will not be flying direct, unfortunately."

"What do you mean?"

"Well, your passport will pick up a few interesting stamps before we go wheels down in Port Harcourt."

"I'm sorry, Mr. Nero, but what does that mean?"

Nero sighed, intentionally slowing so Halifax could catch up. "What it means, Doctor, is that we're flying into a place called Port Harcourt in the Niger Delta. But if we were going to fly direct, it'd be 6,500 miles. Now that's more than twice the distance from New York City to Los Angeles–"

"My lord."

"–and unfortunately, the Bell will only go about 2,800 or so before we're out of petrol."

"Then how will we–"

"First, we fly out to New York. Then we will head up north to Newfoundland, shoot on over the Labrador sea, fill up in Nuuk in Greenland, skip over to Iceland, drop down to London, skip to Bilbao, move south to Casablanca, continue to Laâyoune, oh wait, we're almost there–" Nero interrupted when Dr. Halifax began to speak.

"From Laâyoune we go to Dakar, and from Dakar I should be able to get us into Port Harcourt without much worry. It does, however, all depend on the weather and how I'm feeling at that point. By then, I'm going to be pretty tired, Doctor, let me tell you. It's not helping that I'm taking us around the coast. I expected you'd want to avoid the Sahara at all cost, correct?" He smiled.

Dr. Halifax stammered. "Is this... is this the only way, Mr. Nero?"

The pair having arrived at the hulking silver shape of Bell, he lowered the bags in his hands with a sigh and began opening the cargo hatches. "I'm sorry, madam?"

"What I mean is, is this how you would fly yourself? You said you would avoid the Sahara for my sake, so is there anything else you are doing for my sake?"

Nero took a deep breath. "Well, this will take us the better part of eight days, Doctor. But it is safest," he said in only a marginally patronizing voice.

"Have you spoken to Dr. Max?"

"Yes, I talked to Quincy."

"And he instructed you to take me using the safest route?"

"Well, Doctor, Quincy always wants me taking the safest route."

"Did you take Dr. Brannigan to Nigeria, Mr. Nero?"

Nero laughed. "You've not met Brick, have you Dr. Halifax? Well, you'd best not call him Doctor anything when you meet him. Let me caution you of that."

"Did you, Mr. Nero?"

"No, ma'am, I did not fly Brick to Nigeria. Ol' Brannigan's been on the road for a while now."

From what she'd learned from Quincy Max, Dr. Halifax knew that this Brannigan was a risk-taker, a brave man who put "the mission" and "the greater good" before himself. He was, as they say, a man who threw caution to the wind. On accepting Dr. Max's offer, Liliana Halifax had decided this was the man she'd most need to emulate if she was going to ever see her small cottage near Branford again. She had not thrown her cap into this mythic melee only to become a half-hearted globetrekker.

"How would you take this *Brick* Brannigan were you to fly him from here to Port Harcourt, Nigeria?"

Nero looked her up and down, from her delicate cloche with small peacock feather down to her fashionable high-heeled shoes. When he once again met her eye, he was wary. "Madam, I don't want to be putting you in any kind of troub–"

"Mr. Nero," Halifax interrupted, "Where I'm going, the last thing I'll need to worry about is a difficult commute. So what is the fastest way to Port Harcourt?"

Nero sighed, the ghost of a smile tugging at the corner of his rakish mouth. "Up to Newfoundland and straight over the Atlantic to the Azores. But see, Doc, that's 1,200 miles over nothing but the desolate Atlantic."

"And then from the Azores?"

"Probably from Ponta Delgada in the Azores to Dakar in Senegal. Then straight to Port Harcourt on the Delta."

"That sounds shorter," Halifax said.

"It sounds shorter because it is. But understand, it's more dangerous, Doctor. It puts strain on the engines, it puts strain on me, and it'll put strain on you, too. Quincy told me we need to take the safest–"

"I imagine he did, Mr. Nero. But unfortunately Dr.

Max won't be flying with us. So we'll fly Dr. Brann... er, *Brick* Brannigan's route."

Nero nodded somberly, but in his eye there was also a glint of something different: Respect.

"As you wish, Doctor."

She looked at him as he looked back at her. "Well?" she said finally.

"Well, what?"

"Well, is there anything else, Mr. Nero?"

"I don't believe, Dr. Halifax," he said with a wink. "Oh wait, yes there is." He smiled. "You can sit in the cabin in the back where there's a cot, or if you like you can put up in the cockpit with me. Up to you. Although I have to say, I wouldn't mind the company." He smiled. "Especially from you. Either way, you best board, Doctor, because we'll be in Africa before you know it."

CHAPTER 14: In Which Our Nefarious Profligate Loses Its Head, and Freedom is Found!

Brannigan turned the Luger in his hand and swung, catching the stiff metal of the gun's grip against the Clockwork Man's temple. The harsh clatter of metal on metal was painful to the ears in the small space. A spark or two flew from the machine's steel visage, but nothing else happened. It proceeded, never slowing a step.

"Andrew!" Brannigan shouted, backing up. "Tell me you've good news, my boy!"

Young Caine was dashing about the room, his pale and shaking hands combing every nook and cranny of the great space. Sweat poured down his face in sheets. He turned and bit his lip. "Uh... not yet, Professor!"

"They say patience is a virtue, Andrew," Brannigan said, parrying a slow punch of the Clockwork Man. "However, I fear mine is wearing thin!"

Von Faust had regained his feet and was circling the strange steel creation, cherry-picking jabs and kicks when he could. The machine was unsteady on its feet, yes, but since being toppled the first time, Brannigan had been unable to stop the slow attack.

And they were running out of real estate.

"Von Faust," Brannigan said as he kicked one great

boot and met the solid resistance of the Clockwork creation's thigh. The machine stuttered, but did not fall. "Von Faust!" Brannigan repeated.

"What is it?"

"Hit the beast up high and I will down low. Perhaps our combined efforts can–"

Von Faust kicked high and planted a muddy boot between the machine's "shoulder blades." It rocked forward before righting itself.

"Damn it all, Von Faust! Do you know nothing of teamwork?"

The German shrugged. "I'm a Nazi," he reasoned.

Brannigan sighed and swung one great fist. It hit the plated chest like a wrecking ball, pushing the Clockwork Man backwards. A second punch followed, then a third. On the chest, matte plates of an unknown metal began to twist and dent under the great strain of Brannigan's fists.

Not to be outdone, Von Faust charged. Carrying all the subtlety and grace of a three-legged elephant, he telegraphed his intentions all too well. The Clockwork Man turned with a snap and met the Nazi head-on. One hand closed over Von Faust's throat and it was all it needed. Using the wicked Captain's momentum against him, the machine catapulted Von Faust through the air like a trebuchet, sending him spiraling into Brannigan.

The two men crumbled to the floor in a pile.

"Bloody hell, man. What is wrong with you?" Brannigan asked.

"Me? The great Brick Brannigan, only good enough to soften the landing for an officer of the Third Reich!"

"What? Silence your idiocy, Heinrich!"

"Oh? Well, mind where you are–"

"–you see you foolish numbskull, I didn't–"

"–intention doesn't matter one damnable–"

"–all the grace of a fascist flying through the air. Oh, pardon me!"

"–and that was certainly not necessary, you ham-fisted, meat-headed Yank. I will see that–"

"–your deli-based insults are as stupid as you are, Von Faust!"

"Professor!" Caine interrupted this illuminating academic discourse with a hoarse shout. "There is no way out!"

Brannigan turned, ignoring Von Faust's angry sputtering. "What, my boy?"

Caine was standing at the far wall, back to the hallway from which they'd entered. "I've checked, sir. There's nowhere else to go."

Brannigan closed his eyes and ran a hand through his hair. "We're trapped," he said.

The Clockwork Man continued towards them at a slow but persistent mechanical gait.

"Kicking seems to work well," Brannigan muttered, hoping to buy some time. He stood tall and raised a leg, aiming his great boot for the machine's sternum. "What ho, robot man! Ponder this for a moment!" Brannigan shouted as he launched a great kick.

Two iron reinforced hands closed over Brannigan's ankle, absorbing the force of the kick with nary a misstep, metallic hands locking tight.

Brannigan growled. "Let go, damnable creation!" He twisted, hopping awkwardly on one powerful leg. "Von

Faust! Help me, you mongrel!"

Von Faust barked–yes, barked!–a laugh and scuttled 'round the machine, lowering a shoulder and charging straight into the Clockwork Man's rigid back.

On his first charge, he bounced ineffectually off the machine, reeling.

"Use some elbow grease, Von Faust!" Brannigan shouted, twisting against the Clockwork Man's grip. Slowly, servo-powered legs rose and took steps towards the Professor's immobilized form as it pulled Brannigan's leg towards its chest.

"Von Faust!" Brannigan shouted.

The fascist Captain abandoned his ill-powered charges in favor of spastic kicks, this time connecting with the Clockwork Man's knee. The robot's progress did not falter.

Releasing one mechanical fist from Brannigan's ankle, the machine extended it towards the Professor's bull-like neck.

Brannigan swatted it away and planted an olympian punch on the Clockwork Man's chrome jaw with a resounding *BONG*. Its head snapped back, but in a moment its two diamond eyes were locked back on Brannigan's. The Professor grabbed the robot's wrist and grit his teeth as he struggled to twist the machine's hand away.

It didn't work.

Von Faust charged once more, this time bouncing off the Clockwork Man's back like a fruit fly. Brannigan felt the cold steel hand close over his throat.

"Vnnnn Fssst!" he squeaked.

Now Von Faust, fascist bastard that he was, understood

well-enough that Brannigan and his young partner Andrew Caine were his two best chances of surviving this strange subterranean chamber. That in mind, it didn't take more than a moment for him to decide to engage fully, throwing his life on the line for his nemesis. (In case you wondered, dear reader.)

The Nazi Captain leapt onto the Clockwork Man's back, his two skinny forearms closing and locking around the machine's robotic neck. Hands at the base of the robot's throat, Von Faust began pulling at cords and cables, thick bundles of wires tearing free with spouts of sparks and short spurting jets of oil.

All at once, the hands of the Clockwork Man released Brannigan and the Professor tumbled to the ground, gasping.

Von Faust yelped at the realization that he was now the sole interest of the terrible robotic creation.

"Andrew!" coughed Brannigan. "Help us!"

Young Caine dashed across the broad space, pallid countenance at a loss for how he could dare contribute to the current pugilistic exchange.

"The back wall," Brannigan said, slowly rising to his feet. "Check the back wall, the only place you've yet to fully investigate!"

As Caine ran past the robot and its squirming captive Von Faust, the Clockwork Man side-stepped to block young Caine's path.

"Professor!"

"You've tipped your hand, you wicked bucket of lug nuts!" Brannigan laughed.

At this point, Von Faust was trapped, the hands of the Clockwork destroyer locked over the Nazi's windpipe.

Von Faust–suffocating as he was–found himself hanging limply in front of the machine, unable to mutter the slightest insult or pleading for help.

Not that he had to plead for help. Despite his abhorrent hatred for Von Faust and everything he stood for, Brannigan could not let the fascist die at the hands of the mechanical creation. As young Caine circled the space, trying for a path to slip past the Clockwork Man, Brannigan rounded on it, using his superhuman speed to slip behind the strange machine, all the while reminding himself that the Clockwork Man was nothing more than a human creation.

"You are just a silly wind-up toy!" the Professor shouted as he stepped behind the machine and wrapped his forearms around the Clockwork Man's neck, huge muscles bulging.

"You had the right idea, Von Faust!" he said, "But you were not strong enough!"

Groaning with exertion, Brannigan tightened his grasp around the machine's neck, huge muscles expanding with each passing moment as the servos struggled against the Professor's brute force. Metal squeaked, then creaked, then bent under the unknowable force. Still the machine did not falter. Von Faust's feet kicked helplessly as Brannigan bit down on his lip and closed his eyes, squeezing with every ounce of strength he could muster. Instead of slowing, the Clockwork Man raised its free hand, a series of *clickclickclick*ing transforming one fist into a quickly revolving circular saw. Slowly, the spinning blade approached Von Faust's face.

The Nazi struggled desperately, eyes wide in fear.

Brannigan saw the blade, and pulled harder, his muscles bulging. There was a *ripping* sound as the cotton

96

of his sleeves tore against the astounding breadth of his biceps. *Just a little more,* he thought. He twisted and tugged harder.

And just like that, the Clockwork Man's head popped off.

It tumbled to the ground with a rather understated clatter, taking with it the machine's strength and resolve. Von Faust fell to the floor a moment later.

"Supernatural you are *not!*" Brannigan laughed. "However anticlimactic that may have been," Brannigan commented, "I have to admit, I found it terribly satisfying."

Von Faust sat up, taking ragged gasps. On his neck, the distinctive outline of the machine's hand was visible. Dark blue and black bruises were already spreading.

"You clumsy lout!" Von Faust shouted. "You nearly let that machine tear my head from my shoulders!"

Brannigan picked up the robot's head. "But, as you can see, your head is still attached. Our automated friend was not so lucky." The Professor turned the skull to face him, looking into the lifeless diamond eyes.

"Professor!" Caine shouted. "Here! I think I've found our way out!"

Brannigan tucked the Clockwork Man's skull under his arm like a football and crossed the room to where young Caine stood hunched over the chest from which the strange machine had originally emerged.

"What is it, my boy?"

Caine knelt at the mouth of the chest and slipped his arms inside, hands closing over cleverly disguised iron loops and tugging. In a moment, the false bottom of the chest came free, revealing a passage beneath, leading straight downward.

"Ah, brilliant!" Brannigan shouted. "It seems we've found our escape."

Behind him, Von Faust picked up the Luger from its place in the dirt. He checked the cartridges in the butt of the gun and smiled to see one bullet remaining. He slipped the Luger back into his holster and walked to Brannigan.

"What have you found, Yankee?"

"If you must pigeonhole me by my athletic affiliations, Von Faust," Brannigan said, "For your information, I prefer the White Sox."

"Whatever," Von Faust sighed, hand subconsciously rubbing his throat. "My head was almost removed twice in the past few minutes; I think you would agree that I've permission to be impatient."

"True, true. For a mechanical creation, he did seem to lack ingenuity. But I can't fault him for that, now can I?" Before Brannigan could say more, he was interrupted by the muted blast of dynamite above them.

"Delacroix," he muttered. Turning to Von Faust, he said, "Won't your employer ever back down?"

Von Faust smiled. "Herr Delacroix is persistent, Brannigan. He realizes I am too valuable to let go."

Brannigan laughed. "Yes, Captain, I'm certain it's *you* Black Fang is pursuing with such fervor!" he laughed boisterously as he shifted the metallic skull from one hand to the other. Von Faust only scowled. "Anyway," Brannigan continued. "Down we go, eh?"

With a great leap, Brannigan vaulted the lip of the chest and led the way downward into darkness, carrying the mechanical skull with him all the while.

***

Together, the three unlikely adventurers tumbled into the darkness, seeming to fall endlessly.

Brannigan landed first, rolling to his feet athletically. Caine tumbled in a heap behind him, clambering upright after a moment. Von Faust landed unceremoniously last, lying flat on his stomach on the rocky ground.

"What has happened, Brannigan?" he moaned. "Where are we?"

"Underground, Captain. As to our escape, a boffo performance, Andrew, I have to say." Brannigan led the group forward, his amazing night vision coming quite in handy in the nigh pitch black darkness.

"Where are we going, Professor?"

"Towards the river, Andrew."

"River, Brannigan?"

"Yes, Von Faust. Can you not hear the sound of water?"

In fact, he couldn't see or hear anything. "Um, yes, of course," Von Faust lied.

Into the darkness, the motley crew continued. After a few minutes, the sound of water was as apparent as the faintly growing pale light in the tunnel ahead. Finally, the three men emerged in a narrow room where their path ended at a roaring river.

"What is this, Brannigan?"

The Professor turned to Von Faust. "Some tributary of the Niger, no doubt."

"That river is certain death, sure to lead into a

subterranean nest of crocodiles or pit vipers." Von Faust pointed. "There, that is our way out." Above them was a hole cut deftly in the roof of the cavern, obscured by thick vines and leaves, but apparent nonetheless. Through the dense webbing of foliage, pale light showed through, illuminating the small cave.

From his holster, Von Faust removed his Luger with a maniacal grin. "This is the end of the story for you, Brannigan."

The Professor flashed a brilliant smile and winked, still clutching the Clockwork Man's skull tightly. "Captain Von Faust, don't you understand? My story has just begun!" The great man grabbed young Andrew Caine and leapt into the churning water, the two true adventurers disappearing from view scant moments later and leaving Von Faust standing alone in the otherwise empty cavern.

Von Faust lowered his pistol and returned it to his holster. "Damn you, Brannigan! Damn you!"

CHAPTER 15: In Which Local Cuisine is Sampled–To the Detriment of Our Heroes!

Dr. Liliana Halifax stood in a spartan hotel room overlooking a busy market on the streets of Port Harcourt. The city was small, but still felt crowded, the terribly oppressive humidity making the young Doctor's hair stick to her sweat-dampened forehead. Archibald Nero sat to her left, smoking a cigar and laying weathered playing cards out on a small table in a game of solitaire.

The two had been in Port Harcourt for three days, and very little had happened. Every night, Nero went out, leaving a .25 calibre pistol behind for Dr. Halifax so he could make his mint on dice games with British Colonial soldiers. Generally he returned shortly before dawn, fistfuls of colorful pound notes filling his pockets.

Their days were spent just like this, with Dr. Halifax waiting and Nero playing cards. They had not been speaking much thanks to an ill-advised advance Nero had made on Dr. Halifax under the influence of imported black English beer. At first, Dr. Halifax had simply pushed him off. Thanks to the pilot's persistence, she had finally been forced to resort to more physical dissuasion. Rather than bargain or cajole, she had simply punched him. In all honesty, it was the first punch she'd ever thrown, and after the fact Nero had described it as "a real humdinger."

"Are you hungry?" Nero asked, picking up his cards and shuffling them.

"No," she said. With a sigh, she lowered the curtains against the setting sun and took a seat in a rickety wooden chair against the wall.

"I'm beginning to get... a might peckish," Nero said, smiling. "Would you like me to take you out? I know a few places that make an astounding maafe where Brick and I've eaten once or twice."

"No, thank you, Mr. Nero."

The pilot sighed, and leaned back. From the floor he lifted a sweating glass of palm wine and took a sip. "Listen, Dr. Halifax, I must say, I am really dreadfully sorry for how I acted yesterday evening. I'm not really used to being in close confines with such a... well, *beautiful* lady like yourself." He smiled awkwardly, the English charm returning as he blushed. "I've no excuse, in truth. Nor did I expect that porter to have such a... strong effect on me."

Dr. Halifax squirmed in the uncomfortable chair. This was the second time Nero had apologized to her. The first time she had effectively stonewalled him. She didn't have the heart to do it to the young man again.

"Forgiven, Mr. Nero," she said. "But try it again, and so help me..."

"Aye, Doctor, I promise to be the most perfect gentlemen."

Halifax nodded. "All right. Just remember that."

Their lodgings had been more than awkward, considering they were staying in Brannigan's room. Vacant as it was, the Professor had paid enough to reserve the room for the month, and a few smooth words from

Nero had secured a second key to allow entrance to the room while the two awaited Brannigan's return. A second room was paid on the floor above–most likely for young Andrew Caine–but Nero had cautioned against the young Doctor staying alone in the relatively seedy establishment. She'd taken his advice on the condition that Nero sleep on the sofa, which he had.

Nero nodded. "Expect nothing less." A long moment passed as he shuffled the cards again. Finally he spoke again. "Well... how about now?"

Halifax's face darkened. "Excuse me, Mr. Nero–"

"No, no, no, Dr. Halifax," he smiled. "Dinner. How about *dinner* now, seeing as we're on speaking terms once more?"

Dr. Halifax thought for a moment, although it was hard with the grumblings of her empty stomach. "Maafe, you say?"

"Yes, indeed. Brilliant stuff. Perhaps some palm wine, shuku shuku, efo, caramelized bananas, banga soup, coconut rice, plantains, jollof rice, custard, fried moi moi... the food here is like nothing you've ever dreamed of. Trust me, the best way to experience a place is to eat their food."

The young Doctor smiled, her mind harkening back to the day she and Nero had spent on the Azores and the dishes of *bacalhau* and *sopa de couves* she'd enjoyed at his recommendation. Food-wise, he hadn't steered her wrong yet.

"All right, Mr. Nero," she agreed after a long moment. "My stomach has convinced me, but I'm trusting you," she smiled. "And I'm taking the .25."

Nero laughed. "Lovely."

Smoke filled the dark room, a static-rife radio was buzzing in the corner behind the bar. The romantic exploration of worldly cuisine was everything that Dr. Halifax had hoped it would be, the smoke and .25 pistol in her handbag not withstanding.

"How is the wine?" Nero asked, taking a generous sip.

"It is... strong," Halifax said, grimacing at the taste.

Somewhere behind them, a group of men laughed and Halifax heard the tinkle of coins on a wood table. The clatter of rolling dice soon followed.

"It's made from the sap in palm trees–not surprisingly," Nero smiled.

Halifax nodded at the shadowy rear of the restaurant. "Is this where you come at night when I'm catching up on Yoruba's mythology?"

Nero squirmed. "Here and there," he admitted.

A tall, thin woman with a bright smile appeared with broad plates in hand and a patterned *gele* wrapped around her head. She shared a few hushed sentences with Nero before leaving the plates and disappearing into the kitchen once more.

"This looks remarkable," Dr. Halifax said. "What is it?"

Nero smiled. "As promised we've got fried plantains, jollof rice, potato pepper soup, moi moi, yam porridge, and chicken suya."

"I don't know where to begin, Mr. Nero." She smiled. "Thank you for bringing me out... I don't generally find myself in places such as this."

"Illegal gambling dens in the backstreets of Port Harcourt on the Niger Delta? I imagine you're far beyond your comfort zone, Doctor."

Halifax took a tentative taste of the jollof rice and smiled. "You are right so far, Mr. Nero."

"And what brings you here again?"

Halifax smiled once more. "It's complicated, Mr. Nero. Do you think there is some water I could–"

"Hold on, there's a reason I told you to drink the wine. Or beer. Things with alcohol, all right?"

"Why is that?"

"We're concerned with catching the... uh, jungle runs, yes?"

"Is that–oh, you mean dysentery," Halifax nodded. "Point taken."

"Have you ever been in the field? And I do mean *outside* the country."

"I have been on an archaeological dig in Wales–"

Nero laughed. "Not quite what I meant."

"–and I flew into London at the start of the expedition."

"I don't think you can call any trip that begins in London an expedition, Doctor."

Halifax blushed, glancing over her shoulder at the open storefront that led onto a dark street. In the distance was a mixed symphony of shouting and slow fog horns from ships on the Bonny River. "Yes, Mr. Nero, your point is taken, although even now we're still within the reach of the British Empire, are we not?"

He smiled. "It is true, but West Africa is a might different from Surrey. And what exactly are you doing here, again?"

"You know Dr. Max, correct Mr. Nero?"

"Sure, I know Quincy. As I said, his name's on my checks."

"How well do you know him?"

"Well enough. Why?"

"He... well, Dr. Max told me a little about Drs. Spooner and Brannigan, hinting at what brought Dr. Brannigan here. He was rather persuasive."

Nero nodded, shoveling a large spoonful of chicken suya into his mouth. "I know Quincy well-enough to know the old bastard can wind a tale."

"What do you mean?"

Nero leaned forward over his mostly empty plate (quite the impressive appetite, Halifax noted) and lowered his voice. "Did old Q mention... the Cabal?"

Halifax's eyes widened involuntarily. "Yes!" she said in a forced stage whisper.

Nero shook his head. "I got that whole spiel. Quite a dog and pony show, I must admit. Now he's going on about some allegiance with the German government–"

"You don't believe it, Mr. Nero?"

"Of course not. How can you? Mixed mythologies and religious relics that can destroy the world?"

"But, Mr. Nero, you work for Dr. Max, don't you?"

"Well, of course I do, Doctor, of course I do. But that doesn't mean I subscribe to what he's selling, does it? I fly the planes, captain the ships, and drive the trucks."

"But what do you know about the Cabal?"

"I know it's a truckload full of shite, and that's enough." Nero shook his head dismissively. "I've flown

Brannigan and Spooner to hell and back and I've never seen a shred of anything to make me believe there is some great nefarious organization behind everything."

"If you customarily go on Dr. Max's expeditions, why aren't you with Dr. Brannigan now?"

"Listen, Doctor, Brick was in the jungles of Malaysia, the mountains of Tibet, the deserts of the Gobi, and now the jungles of the Niger delta. As a matter of fact, he's probably been in a few dozen of other places in between. Old Brick may have the temperament of a Benedictine friar, but I, on the other hand, am far from celibate. I need..." He cleared his throat and blushed slightly. "I need... well, *shore leave* occasionally."

Dr. Halifax blushed terribly and re-settled herself in her seat, straightening her blouse. "Mr. Nero," she chided.

"Forgive me, Doctor, I'm just a man!"

"So your desire for... um, *desire* has kept you off many of Dr. Max's expeditions?"

"I have been on my share of jungle treks," Nero admitted. "But I try and keep my boots clean as much as possible. Remember, I'm the pilot and the driver. There are some places that are not fit for transportation, wing or wheel."

"And so you find yourself spending more time in cities? Like Port Harcourt?"

"Absolutely. I have spent time here, in Dakar, Casablanca, Tangier, Carthage, Lagos, Cairo, Kinshasa, Mogadishu, Khartoum. Hell, the list goes on and on. This is truly one of my favorite continents."

"And you've never seen or heard anything that made you believe in the Cabal?"

Nero smiled. "I've fought rebel factions,

revolutionaries, rogue generals, and criminals alike, none of which have ever given a flying banana about the Cabal."

"I'm sorry? A... flying banana?"

"Sorry. Nobody I've ever encountered knows anything of the Cabal. Nor do they give a damn."

Halifax nodded. "Fair enough."

Nero smiled. "But you're going to reserve your judgement, are you?"

"I believe I will, Mr. Nero. Although I would be quite satisfied if this Cabal truly was just a figment of Dr. Max's imagination."

She smiled and took another sip of palm wine, neither Halifax nor Nero realizing how they'd let their voices rise in volume over the past few minutes. Neither did they notice when a bearded man in a dirty, sun-faded shirt nodded ominously to the bartender, rose from his seat at the bar, and slipped silently past a drunken British soldier and out into the hot African night.

All the while, a dastardly grin graced his face. Trouble was certainly afoot!

***

After one final round of palm wine, Archibald Nero led our neophyte adventuress into the insect-filled African night. It was humid, and the dark streets of Port Harcourt were all but deserted. Only a few minutes passed before our amorous Mr. Nero had led Dr. Halifax along a cobblestone promenade overlooking the Bonny River. Perhaps it was her third glass of palm wine, perhaps it was the chirping of the field crickets, perhaps it was the whole adventure carrying her away, or perhaps it was simply the care with which Mr. Nero had led the good Doctor through the evening; whatever it was, she did not object when he wrapped his arm around her waist and pulled her to him.

"Liliana," he said, affecting his suavest tone of voice. "It sure is a lovely evening, isn't it? I am so glad you are here with me."

Dr. Liliana Halifax found herself smiling. Mr. Nero's eyes were lovely, she realized for the second time. "And I you, Mr. Nero. Archibald. I must say, you were right. This continent is truly remarkable."

"Best place on Earth," he reveled. A small fishing boat cruised past as the wily pilot leaned in for a kiss.

Unfortunately, a bullet shot by a poorly trained marksman interrupted our adventurers.

PING! It rang against the iron railing standing between our heroes and the swirling dark waters of the Donny!

"What the devil?" Nero said, pulling away from Dr. Halifax.

"What? Why, Mr. Nero... I mean, um, Archibald... what is it?"

"Did you hear that, Liliana? It was a shot!"

"A shot?"

"Yes, a shot, woman! A gunshot!"

"There's certainly no need for that tone!"

A second shot cut off any need for further discussion.

In a moment, Nero led Dr. Halifax as the two ran through the darkened streets, moving from unevenly paved to unpaved roads, hard-packed dirt to cobblestones. A few vendors remained on the street as well as a handful of musicians and patrons overflowing from bars onto crowded corners. A smattering of British soldiers mixed drunkenly with the locals. None of them offered any help as our heroes ran for their lives!

They passed through crowds of drunkards and overturned one or two tables of mangoes, avocado pears, and grapefruits. All the while, Nero shouted "Clear the way! Clear the way, I say!" while Dr. Halifax begged pardons. She even dropped a few pound notes to one vendor who lost a large number of papayas to stampeding feet.

The only other sound that accompanied them all the while were the gunshots.

Sharp and persistent, at first Nero only heard the small *taptaptap* of a small .22 following them through Port Harcourt's narrow lanes. But when the resounding *BOOM!* of a double barrel felled an unfortunate British soldier, Nero knew they were in real trouble.

"The hotel!" he said as they turned a sharp right. "We need to get back to the hotel! These soldiers are no help. I need my pistol!" A storm of buckshot ripped into a stone facade, coughing up a mouthful of dust a few inches behind Dr. Halifax.

"Take mine!" Dr. Halifax shouted over pistol fire.

"What did you say, Liliana?"

"I said *take mine!*" She pushed the .25 calibre pistol that she had been carrying for her own protection (until that caution went by the way–along with her sobriety!) into his hand and smiled.

In a small traffic circle surrounding a fountain, Nero turned, crouching with Dr. Halifax behind the stone fountain, and took aim.

A pair of armed gents emerged from an alleyway at the

far end of the circle but a few moments later, guns bared.

The tiny .25 barked loudly, emitting nearly no muzzle flash, and sent the pursuers scattering for cover. At the sound of the double-barrel clattering to the ground, Nero laughed.

"Let's go, Liliana! We're almost there, and this is our chance!"

They turned and ran.

Just a minute later found them barging through the front entrance of their seedy hotel, both of them laughing at their narrow escape, their moods buoyed by the palm wine. They pounded up the steps, and pushed into their room, locking their door behind them.

"Perfect," Nero said laughing. "I'd completely forgotten about that damnable .25," he smiled. "You certainly saved the day!"

"Well, I know now you can never be too careful, eh Archibald?"

"I think we're safe," Nero said, pulling back a dirty curtain and looking out over the street below.

"I do hope so, I think the pistol is empty. Now what was that all about do you think?"

"I don't know. Ruffians?" Nero shrugged. "Port Harcourt can be a rough town, Liliana. I should have warned you. It was foolish of me to keep you out so long after dark."

"You don't think..."

"What?"

"Well, you do remember what I said about Dr. Max?"

"Quincy?"

"Yes, what with that Cabal of his? It is why I'm here,

after all."

"Oh, Liliana."

"What?"

"Don't be ridiculous."

"Ridiculous? Why is that ridiculous?"

"I told you, I've never in all my years seen any proof of that Cabal of his."

"I remember, Archibald..."

"So I can't understand how you would put more credence in a fictional secret society than the simple crime known in every large city around the globe. I believe those young men meant nothing more than to rob us."

"Rob us?" Skepticism filled her voice. "They shot at us with a pistol and a rifle, Archibald."

"It was a shotgun."

"Well, whatever it was, I believe it meant business. They killed a Colonial soldier!"

Nero bit his lip and walked back towards her, meaning to finish what he'd started on the promenade. "Don't worry about our pursuers, my dear. They're gone now and we are safe."

She smiled, the blush of the palm wine reddening her cheeks. "Oh is that right?"

Now Nero smiled. "Yes," he said. "That's right."

He leaned in once more when the sound of breaking glass shattered their quiet moment. A gunshot followed and the single lightbulb exploded, plunging the room into darkness.

In the newly darkened room, a pair of bodies crashed through the window. One invader raised an eerily familiar .22 to Dr. Halifax's temple. The second tackled

Nero to the bare wooden floor.

"Blast you!" Nero shouted. "That's the second time we've been interrupted. Can't you appreciate what I'm trying to do here, you fool?"

Apparently, our pair of night raiders could not.

"Mr. Nero," the gold-toothed man standing over Archibald said. "Please be quiet."

"I will not be quiet, you lout, I feel... rather frustrated at the moment!"

"Silence, or your lady friend will be killed."

An ominous cocking of a pistol reinforced this sentiment.

"What the bloody hell do you want?"

"Your cooperation, Mr. Nero," Gold-tooth said. "There is something that we want from you."

"You aren't liable to get it under the threat of murder, you damned ruffian."

Gold-tooth smiled. "You are correct, of course." He turned to his .22 caliber wielding partner. "Jari," he said. "Lower your weapon."

His partner, sweating nervously, nodded and did so. Dr. Halifax breathed a deep sigh of relief. For the moment.

"You see, that was simple," Nero said. "What's with the shooting? We're all civilized people here."

"I needed your attention," Gold-tooth said. "As I said, there is something I need from you that you will not want to give me. I needed your attention because I wanted to show you this." In the darkened room, he raised a small glass vial, faint green liquid just visible in the moonlight.

"And what the devil is that?"

"I believe it is all the motivation you will need to cooperate with us, Mr. Nero," Gold-tooth said with a sharp laugh.

"What do you mean?"

"You see, Mr. Nero, this is the antidote to the poison you drank at my restaurant."

Dr. Halifax gasped.

Gold-tooth smiled broadly.

Mr. Nero did not.

CHAPTER 16: In Which Professors Brannigan and Halifax Finally Meet (Accompanied by the Romantic Soundtrack of Gunfire!)

(5:47:09 until Gold-tooth's poison induces certain death!)

"You have six hours until you expire," Gold-tooth said. "At four hours, your immune system will weaken fatally. After the five hour mark, your nervous system will begin to shut down. By six hours, complete paralysis will have taken hold and you will die."

"Six hours?" Dr. Halifax gasped.

"Perhaps a spot less than that now, Liliana," Nero said, frowning (Indeed, a mere 5:46:55). "What wicked concoction did you give us, you bastard? And why?"

"You have something I want, Mr. Nero," Gold-tooth said. "I believe a simple trade is in order."

"And what would that be?" Nero asked.

"I believe the good Doctor knows," Gold-tooth smiled once more. "It is what brought her here, after all."

Dr. Halifax's eyes widened. "Me?" she said breathlessly. "You want something I have?"

Of course, it only took her a moment to realize that the Gold-toothed gent across from her must be after the disc. *That disc*, she swore to herself. *That damnable disc!*

Curse that stupid relic! Of course! That must be what the fiend is after!

"I've no idea what you're after!" she said with a scowl. "Give us the antidote, you ruffian!"

"Calm yourself, Doctor," Gold-tooth said. "And please, dispense with your lies. If we wait six hours, I'm sure the truth will be bursting from your lips."

She took a different tact. "All right. You must have searched the room, correct? And did you locate it?"

Gold-tooth frowned. Dr. Halifax found the expression terribly satisfying.

"We found nothing," he said. "Yes, we searched."

As if to illustrate this fact, Gold-tooth nodded to his partner Jari who stepped away from Dr. Halifax momentarily to open the closet door. A tumble of clothing and open suitcases spilled across the dark floor.

"You ransacked my possessions!" Dr. Halifax shouted. "Indeed you are a ruffian. Yet if you found nothing, why do you still believe me to be in possession of this... *item*."

"Because our agents in the United States telegrammed confirmation that the Cipher of Dumuzid is in your possession. And agents of the Cabal do not make mistakes."

Simultaneously, Dr. Halifax shouted "Dumuzid?!" as Mr. Nero exclaimed "Cabal?!"

Gold-tooth glanced from once face to the other. "Yes," he said. "You *both* heard me correctly."

"I've no bloody idea what you're on about, you lout, but if you don't give us that antidote, I promise you we'll never cooperate!" Nero sneered.

"Mr. Nero, I've no trouble killing you now, save for

your presence seems to have a... *calming* effect on the lady."

"I resent that," Dr. Halifax said. "Whatever you think was happening prior to your interruption–"

"Liliana, no reason to be angry," Nero began.

"–I assure you, I am a *lady*–"

"Shut up!" Gold-tooth hollered. He turned to Dr. Halifax, and his face hardened. "The Cipher, Doctor."

"And if I say no?"

"I was chosen for this mission because of my solitary abilities of persuasion, Dr. Halifax. My counterparts in your country failed where I will only succeed. Let me assure you, poison is just the beginning. But, seeing as you are new to this, let me begin with the most persuasive tool in anyone's arsenal: logic."

With a slight bow, Gold-tooth gestured to a chair in the corner. "Please, have a seat." Tentatively, Dr. Halifax lowered her raised hands and sat.

"The Cipher is useless alone, Doctor. In giving it to me, you forfeit nothing. Nothing will come to harm. It is, alone, worth nothing. Harmless. Void of danger or threat. The only threat present is that on your own life. Yours and the good Mr. Nero's. What say you to that?"

"If it is so worthless," Dr. Halifax asked, "then why do you want it so desperately?"

"I serve at the pleasure of my Master. Today, he asked me for the Cipher of Dumuzid. So here I stand before you, ready to make a deal to trade your life in exchange for a worthless relic."

Relic. The word jarred Dr. Halifax's memory. She remembered Quincy's words and could think of nothing but the threat the Cabal posed against her small blue world.

Frightened more than she'd perhaps ever been in her life, Dr. Halifax forced herself to smile. "I will never give it to you," she said.

From the darkest shadow of the room, a booming baritone voice said, "That's the spirit, doll!"

Gold-tooth turned, eyes wide as a fist approximating the size of the moon smashed into his face. A moment later, his eponymous gold tooth clattered to the floor in a spattering of blood droplets.

Before his partner Jari could draw his .22, the fist struck again, knocking the young man sideways.

"Brannigan!" Nero shouted. "The antidote!"

"Antidote? What? What did I miss? I've only just arrived! Andrew! Get him!"

From the floor, Mr. Sans Gold-tooth rose and stumbled to the shattered window from whence he'd entered and leapt through it, beating a hasty retreat. In the darkness, Dr. Halifax saw a grand silhouette take shape, leaping through the window frame in pursuit. Behind him, a young man tackled the already prone shape of Jari, struggling to pin his limp arms behind his back.

"Stay here, Liliana," Nero shouted as he pulled a box of matches from his coat. With a snap, a match came to life, casting a soft gold glow over the dark room. "Andrew will protect you!"

"Andrew?" Dr. Halifax asked, her eyes resting on the young man fighting with an unconscious body on the floor. "This boy?" She turned as Nero disappeared out the window in pursuit of Brannigan and Gold-tooth.

"To hell with that!" she shouted, following the two adventurers.

She did not hear when Andrew said, "You'll all leave me alone with this brute?"

***

She landed on a flat tarred roof. Ahead of her, Nero pursued the large man she suspected to be Professor Brannigan. In the soft light of the stars, she made out the shapes of the three men as they jumped across the chasm between the flat tarred roof of the hotel and the bowed wooden roof of the adjacent building.

"Buckle up, Liliana!" she said to herself as she took off after the three men. "And whatever you do, don't look down!"

Her knee-high leather boots scuffed against the tar beneath her feet as she sprinted to the roof's edge. Gritting her teeth, she didn't slow as she reached the jagged edge and leapt.

She flew across the emptiness with all the grace of an eagle. The distance seemed infinite.

She crashed to a landing on the old wooden roof as the three men ahead of her neared the far edge of the building. Beneath her feet, the roof sagged ominously, accompanied by the frightful sound of beams cracking.

A gunshot sliced through the air as Gold-tooth fired over his shoulder at his three pursuers.

"Fire away, you buffoon!" the baritone voice shouted in the cricket-filled night. "You will not escape justice!"

A second shot filled the air as Gold-tooth leapt from the roof onto the next building, a high, peaked clay tile roof. Soon, Brannigan followed with Nero at his heels.

Dr. Halifax scurried across the old wooden roof, the sound of wood cracking growing louder as each step became less sure beneath her feet. She jumped onto the stone ledge of the building as the roof behind her cracked and gave way in an avalanche of rotten wood.

The gulf before her was immense, an expansive darkness between her and the next building. Below her, the street eagerly awaited a plunging body.

"Don't look down, don't look down, Liliana!" she reminded herself (perhaps a few moments too late). "You can do this. I *know* you can do this."

She swung her arms in a great circle to gain momentum before throwing her body across the great abyss.

She made the leap with all the skill of a gold medal Olympic long jumper.

Landing, however, was another story.

Her boots hit the peaked clay tiles with a *CRASH!* and her footing gave way beneath her. With a sharp gasp, she slid, her body tumbling backwards towards the edge. Above her, the shapes of the three men struggled to climb the sharp, peaked roof, shattered tiles rolling down the gradient towards her.

Her boots dug into the flimsy metal gutter, finding purchase and interrupting her soon-to-be-fatal descent. Dr. Halifax turned her attention away from the empty cobblestone street–two stories below–and back at the chase above her. The elusive Professor Brannigan had caught up to Gold-tooth at the peak of the roof, and as Nero struggled to reach the top, the Professor and the hooligan tangled in a barrage of fisticuffs. Great impacts sounded, knuckles on flesh, bones cracking, grunts and roars.

"Hurry, Archibald!" Dr. Halifax shouted as a glint of moonlight heralded the entrance of a long knife into the game. Gold-tooth smiled and lashed out.

Cloth tore and Brannigan shouted an obscenity as he fell backwards. Gold-tooth closed on him, turning the blade in his hand so the point lanced downward like a great canine tooth, ready to make the killing plunge.

Nero jumped–barely far enough to reach Gold-tooth– and wrapped his arms around the ruffian's leg. The man stumbled, arms pinwheeling for balance. As the knife-wielding madman prepared to bury his blade in Nero's neck, the wily pilot swung a British fist and buried it deep in the attacker's kidney.

Gold-tooth shouted and fell to one knee. A clatter of metal on clay pulled Dr. Halifax's eye away from the flurry of action on the peak of the roof.

A pistol tumbled down the clay towards her. Unsteadily, she shifted her feet and reached, the small silver gun threatening to slide past her and tumble to the street below. She extended herself as far as she could, the metal gutter groaning beneath her. All at once, she realized it was simply too far, the pistol was to escape her. Not to be foiled by the tenacity of gravity, however, she jumped.

Arm fully extended, she caught the pistol just before it fell over the edge of the building. Unfortunately, there was nothing for *her* to land on.

And so, over she slipped.

Now, in such a situation, your average non-adventurer would almost certainly plunge to their death. Dr. Liliana Halifax, however, was *not* your average non-adventurer. As we learned in Chapter 13, Dr. Liliana Halifax was no mere professor anymore. She was an adventuress, and little did she know that the blood running in her veins came from a long line of adventuresses going back to her great-great-great-grandmother. But that is another sub-plot for another tale. All you need to know now is that Dr. Liliana Halifax was made from, well, much stronger stuff than she could even begin to fathom.

So, over she did slip, yes, but she was saved. Saved by *herself*, that is.

Hanging from one hand, nickel-plated pistol clutched in one hand, she turned her attention to the three men grappling on the peak of the roof.

The fierce Gold-tooth (also built from stronger stuff than either Brannigan or Nero could begin to fathom, apparently) was still putting up one hell of a fight. At his feet, Nero was smote, metal heel of the knife having cracked against the Brit's temple, leaving him little more than an unconscious lump. Brannigan was back on his feet, his huge form silhouetted against the moon as he struggled to prevent the knife from burying itself into his heart. Gold-tooth gritted his teeth in a mad scowl as the two men matched muscle for muscle in the moonlight. Slowly, the point of the knife approached the bulging muscles of Professor Brannigan's chest.

The perfect point of the knife was three inches away. Two inches. One inch.

Brannigan howled as the knife *slowly* slipped into his flesh.

"No!" Dr. Halifax shouted. She had to do something. But what?

Brannigan felt the cold steel of the fierce ruffians blade cut into his skin like a hot poker. Blood ran down his filthy khaki shirt. "You... *bastard!*" he grunted.

A pistol shot cracked through the night, and in the light of the moon, a spray of blood filled the air.

Gold-tooth fell to his knees and tumbled down the roof, end over end, hand over foot, head over tail, etc, etc.

Lifelessly, he rolled over Dr. Halifax (hanging as she was from her one slight hand) and fell the two stories to the ground below. He landed with a terribly wet *crunch*. The good Doctor could not help but look down in horror at the gruesome mess below her. That was her doing! And yet... it needed to be done, didn't it? She'd saved that man's life. That... *Brick Brannigan*.

She looked up and saw, for the very first time, a devilishly handsome face, perfectly illuminated by soft Nigerian moonlight, staring down at her, a twinkle in his eye.

The devilishly handsome face of none other than Brick Brannigan!

"Thank you, my dear," he said with a gentle yet debonair smile. "I owe you my very life."

CHAPTER 17: In Which Our Adventurers Are Informed of the Inevitability of Their Deaths!! And at the Hands of Their Savior, Nonetheless. Good Grief...

(4:02:11 until Gold-tooth's poison induces certain death!)

Dr. Liliana Halifax was seated on a plush, red velvet settee, tapping one booted foot on the well-polished wood floor and trying not to dwell on either her impending death or the fact that she had just shot a man.

She stopped tapping her foot and asked, "Anything?" I believe it was the eleventh or twelfth time she'd asked.

The man know as Brick Brannigan–seated at an otherwise empty bar–leaned back, removed his large blue eye from his stethoscope, and smiled. Despite the poison strolling through her veins, leading her towards a premature doom, Dr. Halifax could feel her heart skip a beat.

"I'm sorry," he said, his voice gentle. "I've news, but none of it good."

Nero quit his pacing and took a seat beside Dr. Halifax, snaking one arm over and around her shoulder quite casually. It would seem, Liliana realized, that poison or no poison, Mr. Archibald Nero was not to be dissuaded in certain pursuits.

"Well, out with it, Brick. What do we need for the cure?"

Before we hear that, dear reader, why don't we backtrack momentarily, following up on the tribulations our adventurers faced during the previous chapter? Currently, they have returned to the grand Hotel Port Harcourt to alter their fates–which have chosen to deal them quite a few nasty hands, if I may say.

Moments after Dr. Halifax had saved Brannigan's life on the rooftops over Port Harcourt, he returned the favor in kind, climbing down to rescue her from her precarious position (dangling from the gutter). Soon after, our three adventurers–a good slap to Nero's British cheek rousted him from his less-than-conscious state–climbed down from their place atop the peaked roof and found themselves staring forlornly at the messy remains of their poisoner.

And what little remained of the antidote!

"Odin's blood!" Brannigan had exclaimed. "It's ruined, it is!" He'd knelt and picked up the small shattered glass ampule. "You said you were poisoned, right Nero? I came into that conversation a few moments late, I'm afraid."

The Brit pilot opened his mouth to respond when Brannigan bowled him over, continuing, "I would imagine that this minuscule vial held your cure, no?"

Nero nodded glumly.

With great care, Brannigan had slipped what remained of the ampule into his breast pocket, careful to keep the small container upright lest he spill any trace of antidote that remained.

He stood and smiled, raised one finger and pointed it skyward as he said, "To the laboratory!"

Nero had only squinted at the Professor as if the great man had begun speaking in tongues. "Laboratory, Brannigan? What are you on about? We're in the jungles of Africa, your room is equipped only with one single lightbulb, what laboratory could possibly–"

"Of course that's not my *true* room, Nero," Brannigan had scolded. "What kind of rube do you think I am?" He looked at Dr. Halifax, eyes glinting in the moonlight, and shook his head as if the two shared some great secret at Nero's expense.

"Your *true* room?" Nero asked, baffled.

Brannigan had smiled. "Please, my friends, follow me."

A few short minutes later, our intrepid adventurers had climbed the stairs of Hotel Port Harcourt and passed the open door that partially blocked the room Nero and Dr. Halifax had believed to be Brick Brannigan's.

"Uh, Professor Brannigan?" Dr. Halifax ventured. "Is this not your–"

"Upward, Doctor," Brannigan said with a smile. "Two more flights."

Soon, they stood outside the door to what was called the King's Suite. Brannigan had pulled a long iron key from his pocket and unlocked double doors leading into the great suite of rooms. The mouths of Halifax and Nero fell open in shock.

The definition of opulence! And equipped with Brannigan's own cavalcade of scientific instruments, nonetheless! Chandeliers and plush furniture; potted palms and crystal glasses; a grand bar for entertaining, replete with brandy and gin; and three bedrooms, each with a luxurious king-sized bed. On the wall opposite the bar, great windows overlooked the Bonny River, sparkling in the moonlight.

"Damn you, Brick," Nero smiled. "And to think the man at the desk had us sleep in your *other* room for those nights."

Now, at this point, dear reader, it should be noted that Brannigan's brow darkened–however marginally–at the mention of "shared nights." His gaze had moved from Nero to Dr. Halifax and back to Nero where it lingered momentarily.

Finally, he said, "I instructed my good man Chuka to do exactly that, Nero. It keeps the riff raff from killing me in my bed at night."

"Chuka?" Nero asked.

"Hotel Port Harcourt's owner and proprietor. You would have met him when you attempted to check in?"

Nero nodded. "Ah, yes. And how do you curry such favors with the locals?"

"I've done favors for Chuka, and he repays me in kind. He is a good man. As a matter of fact, I introduced him to his wife."

Nero laughed. "And I imagine you have lairs such as this in nearly every port?"

Brannigan had smiled. "Nearly."

"And you never told me?"

The Professor shrugged. "What kind of secret remains a secret when shared with you, Nero?"

At this, the Brit had only scowled, belying the rather fuzzy current state of the two adventurers' relationship.

"Anyway," Brannigan had said. "Make yourselves a drink, and have a seat." He gestured to the great oak bar that flowed along the eastern wall, upon which sat his large microscope and chemistry kit. "Only time is needed now."

And so, time passed. Too much time, if you asked Dr. Halifax. She sat on the settee while Nero paced. It was a frustrating parade of minutes that eventually bore only bad news, which brings us to where we stood prior to our trip back in time.

"Bad news, you were saying?" Dr. Halifax reminded.

Brannigan nodded. "I believe the Cabal–"

"Ack, the Cabal!" Nero interrupted. "Balderdash!"

"What? Why you heard the man, Archibald," Dr. Halifax said. "That gold-toothed fellow freely *admitted*–"

"That's... that's nothing to do with it!" Nero said angrily. "I still don't believe it."

"Perhaps you will believe this, Nero," Brannigan said, turning on his barstool to face the Brit. "Do you believe the two gentlemen who attacked you and the good Doctor to be international criminal masterminds?"

"International criminal masterminds?" Nero asked. "Are you barmy?"

"Yes, international criminal masterminds. No, I am not 'barmy,' as you say."

"Don't be ridiculous, Brannigan. Those men were nothing but local hooligans!"

Brannigan nodded sagely and smiled. "I thought you would say as much. Unfortunately for you and Dr. Halifax, you are wrong."

"What do you mean?"

"Had these two men been local hooligans, they would surely have poisoned you with venom of the West African carpet viper. You see, the West African carpet viper–or *echis ocellatus*, if you will–is one of the deadliest snakes in the whole world. Based on sheer convenience, I'm certain your local hooligans would use this poison, wouldn't you say?" Nero nodded. "Yes. Well, this poison," Brannigan said, gesturing at the slide beneath his microscope, "is not that of the West African carpet viper. In fact, it is not even from this region."

Nero screwed his face up. "What do you mean, Brannigan? Where is it from? *East* Africa?"

"Unfortunately no. I say 'unfortunately' because were it from this continent, I most assuredly could cure it with local remedies. Not only is it not from Nigeria, neither is it from this continent or even this hemisphere."

"What?" Nero's eyes widened in shock.

"And so...?" Dr. Halifax began, her pallor draining.

"There is nothing I can do with what is at my disposal here in Port Harcourt," Brannigan said. "And when you factor in the exotic exceptionality of this poison, I do believe it points to a global organization akin to the Cabal." He smiled, quite satisfied with his deduction.

"To hell with the Cabal," Nero sputtered. "The poison, Brannigan, the poison!"

"We are to... die of this poisoning?" Liliana interrupted, her voice hoarse. "In but a few hours?"

Brannigan smiled. "Now, I didn't say that, my dear," he said, not unkindly. "I can save you from the poison, although in order to do that, I will have to..."

"Yes, Brannigan?" Nero said, his own eyes betraying the fear he felt deep in his soul.

The ease with which Brannigan replied made our two poison victims shiver. "To save you," he said, "I will have to kill you."

"Kill...?"

"Well... in a way." From a medical satchel, Professor Brannigan pulled a long, glass-bodied syringe. The needle at the end of the syringe was long, perhaps three inches.

"What is that?" Nero asked breathlessly.

"It is your death–and your salvation," Brannigan said. "It is a rare toxin that must be delivered straight to the heart. I hope you've each made your peace," he said with a mischievous grin.

Dr. Halifax and Nero looked a right pair of ghosts, I can tell you that!

Professor Brannigan, on the other hand, was enjoying himself terribly.

"Now," he said. "Who would like to go first?"

CHAPTER 18: You Need Answers, Dear Reader? Well, So Do Liliana and Archibald, So Here They Come! (Beware the Golden Lancehead!!)

(3:41:57 until Gold-tooth's poison induces certain death!)

"Damnit, Brannigan, wait!" Nero shouted. "We need answers, for God's sake!"

Brannigan opened his mouth to speak when he was interrupted by the banging of the suite's door opening. The three adventurers turned in unison to see Andrew Caine–Brannigan's young partner, remember?–elbow the door open breathlessly. Lying prostrate on the floor at his feet was Gold-tooth's still-unconscious partner Jari.

"Ah, yes, I'd almost forgotten, Andrew," Brick said with a smile. "Dragged him up here? Well done!"

Struggling to catch his breath, young Caine only nodded his head.

Brannigan slipped from his stool and crossed the room. In the doorway, he lifted unconscious Jari like a sack of potatoes and carried him to a spare couch. With nary a grunt, he deposited Jari dismissively onto it before turning his attention back to Nero and Dr. Halifax.

"Where was I?" he asked himself.

"Answers, Professor Brannigan?" Dr. Halifax

suggested. "I believe you were going to give us... a bit more information."

"Yes, of course. Apologies." Brannigan scratched his head and resumed his seat at the bar. "The poison," he said, once again gesturing to his microscope. "Is incredibly rare."

"How rare, Brannigan?" Nero asked.

The great Professor shifted on the stool and smiled sheepishly. "There is an island very far away off the coast of São Paulo in Brazil. Now this small place is, well, legendary not only because of how remote it is, but also because civilians are banned from it. People are banned because there is a rare pit viper found only on the island. This snake gives the island the name for which it is today known: *Snake Island*."

"If this... Snake Island is truly as remote as you say, how is it that you recognize its venom as it courses through our veins?" Nero asked.

Brannigan smiled. Still huffing and puffing, young Caine seated himself beside the Professor and forced a smile himself.

"That is a story for another day," Brannigan said. "Suffice to say, the Brazilian Navy is not the security force they believe themselves to be!"

"You've been there?" Dr. Halifax asked. "And the venom, you studied it?"

Brannigan nodded. "I did indeed. I made good friends with Lucas Rocha, the lighthouse keeper. His affinity for *Truco Paulista* made us quick friends."

"But the venom, Brannigan!" Nero urged. "Damnit, man, stay on topic!"

"Yes, of course. The venom of the golden lancehead–

the snake known only to Snake Island–is not always deadly in and of itself. Unfortunately, your blood samples have both shown that the poison you're inflicted with to be a mixture of the lancehead venom and *Acontium*. You may better know *Acontium* by its other names: Monkshood, wolf's bane, the queen of poisons, and half a dozen others. Suffice to say, you two have quite a nasty concoction flowing through your veins."

"And you said something about... killing us?" Dr. Halifax asked, her voice soft. She did not want to admit it to her brave companions–nor herself–but she felt a great deal of fear. Her first adventure, also to be her last? And all because of a dinner shared with... Archibald Nero? Good lord. She shivered. *Nero*? What on Earth had come over her? She took a deep breath and looked at Brannigan, trying to be brave. As many young adventurers and adventuresses can tell you, it's hard to be strong when your proverbial chips are down.

"I was merely being theatrical, Dr. Halifax," Brannigan said, rising from his stool and coming towards her. "A thousand apologies. But theatricality aside, what must be done is indeed dangerous." He took a seat across from her and smiled, hoping to allay her fears, even marginally.

"And what is that, Brannigan?" Nero asked. Even the wily British pilot looked stricken at this point.

"It is true there is no cure for what has afflicted each of you–*here*. There is no cure *here*. If we are able to fly out of Port Harcourt and travel to Tangier, we will be able to locate the means and resources to save both of your lives."

Dr. Halifax smiled, relief blooming on her face. Nero, on the other hand, looked crestfallen.

"Tangier?" he said, leaping to his feet. "*Tangier*? But Brannigan... that's over three *thousand* miles away! It would be faster to cross the United States! And here we would be flying over dense jungles and barren deserts. How long did that gold-toothed bastard say we had before our bodies would begin to shut down?" Face pale, Nero looked at his wristwatch. "Good lord!"

"By my count," Brannigan said, "you've only about three and one half hours."

"Three and a half hours! We will never make it to Tangier in that time!" The once-brave Brit pilot collapsed on a barstool beside young Andrew Caine and grabbed at a bottle of brandy. Yanking the cap, he poured a few fingers into a cut crystal glass and downed it greedily.

"Nero," Brannigan said. "Calm down, you're acting mad. And you're scaring the lady."

Dr. Halifax didn't hear the kind–albeit patronizing– words. She was busy staring off into space, contemplating her own premature ends and cursing the day she signed for that blasted package.

The package! Once again, Quincy Max's words brought her back to Earth. She could not be frightened. She was trusted with a mission, and poison be damned, she was going to complete it successfully.

She stood. "Professor Brannigan," she said, interrupting the Professor's attempts at calming Nero. "I have something to deliver to you."

"Uh, deliver?"

"Deliver?" Nero squawked. "Didn't you hear? We're *dying*!"

"Shut up, Nero," Brannigan chided. "I can save you, I told you!"

"Can you tell time, Brannigan? Do they teach *that* at Yale?"

"I didn't go to Yale, I went to Oxford, Harvard, Cambridge–"

"Brick," Dr. Halifax said, stopping the great man mid-sentence. "Back at Branford University, I received a package from Dr. Spooner. It is this package that brought me here in the first place."

"And signed our death warrant!" Nero said.

On any other day, Brannigan would have had some choice words for the pilot, but at this moment, he could think nothing more than *I sure do like the way my name sounds when coming from the lips of this beautiful woman.*

"Yes, Doctor?" Brannigan said. Unconsciously he reached out and took her hand, helping her to her feet. "Show me." Her hand was small in his.

She smiled, feeling the fear and anxiety drop away like the shedding of an uncomfortably wet raincoat. She stood. "It's downstairs."

"Where are you going?" Nero asked, taking a deep gulp of brandy. "Didn't you hear that bit about our deaths?"

As Brannigan and Dr. Halifax walked past him towards the door, young Andrew leaned over and said to Nero, "Here's what's going to happen, Arch..."

***

In the dark room two floors below, Brannigan lit a candle to chase away the shadows. He held it high and said, "Where did you hide it, Doctor?"

Slight beside his great stature, Dr. Halifax put her hands on her hips and looked around. After the tussle, it was a right mess.

135

"Archibald and I arrived here only days ago, searching for you. I came because Dr. Max convinced me to deliver what I received."

"That explains why you were in my room," Brannigan said. "I've come to expect finding Archibald at a moment's notice, but generally he is not with such... remarkable company."

In the darkness, Liliana blushed. "I'd not met Mr. Nero prior to setting off, and I have found his company rather mawkish when not annoying."

Brannigan laughed heartily. "Perfectly put, Doctor. I am relieved to hear it. If we're being honest, I had feared you one of his trollops!"

It was Dr. Halifax's turn to laugh. Part of her may have taken offense, but there was something in his voice that did indeed speak of true relief. "Fortunately for me, I am not–despite his best efforts. All those efforts gained him were a punch in the nose and three nights sleeping on *that*." She pointed at a small love seat, not nearly large enough for a full grown man to rest on.

Brannigan quite enjoyed that visual (at Nero's expense).

"Anyway," Dr. Halifax continued, "Upon arriving, I sensed that discretion was well-advised, so I hid the package I'd been trusted with."

Taking a knee before a small cabinet at the bedside, Dr. Halifax tugged the piece of furniture away from the wall. At her side, Brannigan knelt.

"Good thinking, Doctor. That foresight no doubt saved your life. If this item had been located, you surely would have been killed in your sleep. No one would have taken the trouble to poison you unless they needed information."

The thought made Dr. Halifax shiver once again.

"I'm terribly sorry to be morbid," Brannigan said, resting a comforting hand on her back. Liliana smiled despite herself, realizing how much *better* Brannigan's hand felt than Nero's.

"It's all right," she said. Her entire life, she'd always hated being coddled, even coming from Brannigan. "This," she said, pulling up a loose floorboard, "is what everyone has been after."

From the dark opening in the floor, Dr. Halifax's small hand removed the leather-bound package that had come so far. With a sigh, she handed it over to Brannigan, trading with him for the candle. Carefully, very carefully, he unwrapped it.

Under the gentle, flickering light of the candle, the disc looked even more remarkable. Brannigan sucked in a breath of air and held it. "Beautiful," he said. "And it is flawless. It is... the Cipher of Dumuzid! And you've protected it, bringing it all this way. Thank you, Doctor!"

Still blushing, the good Doctor said softly, "Please, call me Lily."

Brannigan smiled, turning his eyes from the remarkable disc to the even more remarkable thing beside him. "Dr. Lily Halifax," he said. "My name is Hugo Brannigan."

Gently, they shook hands. "It is a pleasure," she said.

"The pleasure is all mine, Lily," he said. "And let me assure you, poison or no poison, I will take care of you. No harm will come to you while my heart still beats." *And beat it does*, he realized. *It beats three times faster when she is near.*

Looking into his eyes, she could do nothing but trust him. Still smiling, she nodded. "Thank you, Hugo."

Who is to say what may have happened next–the two adventurers sharing such a once-in-a-lifetime moment over a priceless mythological relic under the romantic glow of candlelight–had the near-hysterical screeching voice of Archibald Nero not interrupted, echoing down the two flights of stairs from the King's Suite above, wailing "HE REALLY IS GOING TO KILL US? HOLY HELL!!"

CHAPTER 19: Hold on Now... Back to That Bit About You Killing Us? Is This Really Necessary? (Why, As a Matter of Fact, It Is). Also, Let's Briefly Meet Jari!

(3:28:01 until Gold-tooth's poison induces certain death!)

When Professor Brannigan and Dr. Halifax burst through the open doors of the King's Suite–both looking a bit flushed, in sooth–they found no wretched murderer standing over the dead bodies of young Andrew and Nero. Hell, they found no dead bodies at all.

Instead, they found Nero pouring himself yet another tall glass of brandy (his hand shaking) with Andrew trying to calm him with rushed words.

"Andrew," Brannigan said disapprovingly, "I had hoped I would be the one to explain the full extent of the plan to Mr. Nero!"

"I'm sorry, Professor!" Andrew said. "It's just that he kept going on and on about dying–"

"–that the young lad decided to *calm* me by explaining how you were going to *KILL* me, Brannigan!"

"Have a seat, my dear," Brannigan said to Dr. Halifax with a smile. "This will only take a moment, I hope." He passed the Cipher to her and walked across the plush

Persian rug to Nero at the bar where he snatched the glass of brandy from the frightened pilot's hand.

"That's enough, Archibald, I believe you need no more brandy today." With one tip of his hand, Brannigan finished Nero's brandy himself before spiriting away the bottle and restoring it to the shelf behind the great oak bar. "Now have a seat." When Nero opened his mouth to protest, Brannigan insisted, "*Now.*"

The pilot sat despondently.

"As my young colleague has already explained to Mr. Nero," Brannigan began, "I'll explain to you, my dear Lily." He smiled at Dr. Halifax.

From a seat adjacent to hers, Nero said incredulously, "Lily?"

Dr. Halifax readjusted herself on the seat and said, "Go on, Hugo."

"*Hugo?*" Nero continued, his eyeballs dangerously close to tumbling out of his skull.

Brannigan cleared his throat. "Yes, a deadly mix of poison flows through your veins. Yes, I am aware of the temporal logistics in getting us from Port Harcourt to Tangier. No, this is not insurmountable. Yes, it will require certain... *finagling* that is slightly... worrisome in theory. No, it will not result in your death."

Nero stared at Brannigan. Finally, he said, "Please explain this 'finagling' that is necessary to prevent our deaths from poisoning. I'm sorry for my hysteria, I am just... well, frightened. Perhaps your young assistant is less delicate than you, Brick."

The Professor nodded. "Thank you, Archibald. Now, using a special mixture of toxins from the far east including trace amounts of a... uh, substances known as tetrodotoxin and bufotoxin, I will slow your physiological processes down to a nearly stationary rate. Once this occurs, I can freeze your bodies to halt the metabolization of the poison, giving me enough time to transport you via plane from here up the coast to Tangier. When I am ready with the cure, I will be able to unfreeze your bodies and inject you with a strong medication that will restart your heart and restore you to current functionality in time for me to cure your poisoning. Simple, no?"

Only silence responded to the Professor's explanation.

After a terribly long time, Nero said, "No, you are no more delicate than your associate."

"You will stop our hearts, freeze us, transport us 3,000 miles, unfreeze us, and bring us back to life?" Dr. Halifax said. She seemed to have a hard time comprehending even her own words.

"Yes, put succinctly, that is true," Brannigan said. "But–"

"And you did say 'tetrodotoxin' and 'bufotoxin'? Is that right? Bufotoxin is toad venom and tetrodotoxin is a neurotoxin with no known receptor antagonist. It is essentially unstoppable once entered into the bloodstream, Hugo." The good Doctor spoke with a rather scandalized tone. "Are you certain this will–"

"Lily," Brannigan said softly. "I've used this on myself. The second chemical mixture is only to bring you from your frozen state, I've taken the toxin mixture to feign death before; it has saved my life more than once and I would not subject you to it if I was anything but certain of its success. The only question is: do you trust me?"

Well. It seemed a might early in our adventurers non-existent relationship to be asking such a terribly heady question, but there it was.

141

Looking into the great Professor's eyes, the answer was clear to Liliana Halifax.

"Yes," she said. Little did it matter that the only alternative was succumbing to poison, that fact was far from her mind. What mattered was the truth, and the truth was she *did* indeed trust Hugo Brannigan with her life.

Archibald Nero was another story.

"I don't!" he said. "At least, not that much!"

"Arch," Brannigan said with a smile. "We've been around the world together. And while we've not always gotten along, we've trusted our lives to each other and lived to fight another day, have we not?"

Nero nodded. "I guess we have, yes."

"So why not trust me now, friend?"

"Well..."

"And what other option do you have? Death to the golden lancehead venom? Plus, it will make a hell of a story to tell the ladies."

Nero's face steeled. "You're bloody right it will, Brick!" He stood up and put his hands on his hips. "By Jove, let's do it!"

***

But first!

(3:18:43 until Gold-tooth's poison induces certain death!)

"Wake up. Wake up, I say!"

Nero was patting Jari roughly on the cheek. The young Nigerian man was still unconscious on the couch, hands tied behind his back. Elsewhere in the King's Suite,

Brannigan, Dr. Halifax, and young Caine were busying themselves packing what was necessary. Mr. Chuka had just departed the room with various instructions from Brannigan, promising to return shortly with everything required. While everyone was preparing for their imminent departure, Nero decided to do what was in his power to be done: question that Jari bloke!

The young man opened his eyes, blinking them repeatedly, slowly clearing a fog. After a moment, he turned and found himself staring up at Nero.

"Good evening," Nero said.

"Oh," Jari said.

"Indeed," Nero smiled.

Nero grabbed the scalawag's shirt and pulled him upright on the plush couch. Jari blinked some more, perhaps not believing what he was looking at.

"You're... still alive?" he asked.

"For the moment," Nero said. "More than I can say for you, you bastard!"

"And Abassi?"

Nero cocked his head. "That the bloke with the gold tooth?"

Jari nodded.

"Fortunately for him," Nero said, "he is dead. If you're looking to escape that, I'd start talking."

"I cannot," Jari said, shaking his head. Beads of sweat had begun to appear on his forehead and top lip.

"Why?"

"They will do worse than kill me."

"They who?"

"The... the Cabal!"

143

Damn, Nero thought. *So it is real. After all this time I had refused to believe.*

"And what is worse than killing you, my friend?" Nero asked.

"Killing my wife and my baby girl. Faraa."

Nero considered his words. After a long moment, he took a seat on a chair across from Jari. "Fair enough," Nero said.

To explain, dear reader, Archibald Nero is a great many things: adventurer, ladies' man, wisecracker, gambler, drinker, sometimes coward (perhaps). But he was not a cruel man, and he understood young Jari–at least in some fashion.

"What can you tell me, Jari?"

The young Nigerian looked confused. "Sir?"

Nero smiled and shook his head. "I'm not going to kill you, son," he said. "But I would appreciate a little give and take, eh?"

Jari exhaled heavily, relief overcoming his face. "Thank you, sir!" he said.

"Don't thank me yet, and don't call me sir, either. Just tell me what you can."

"About... the Cabal?" The young man shivered. "I was forced to work with Abassi. Forced on penalty of death. You see, they are *beasts*," he whispered. "I've heard that they eat the flesh of men; each member of the Inner Circle has thirteen lives; the Master can breathe fire and walk on water. They wish to... *destroy the world.*"

Nero leaned forward. "Be straight with me, Jari," he said. "Start at the beginning. Tell me... *everything.*"

***

144

(3:03:22 until Gold-tooth [henceforth known as Abassi]'s poison induces certain death!)

Jari talked, and Nero listened. And when Chuka knocked once more on the doors to the grand King's Suite, our adventurers were ready. Together they walked downstairs to the lobby, each carrying a leather bag packed with what they needed–Dr. Halifax silently lamenting leaving the majority of her substantial luggage behind. Brannigan carried a weary leather satchel across his chest inside of which lay the Cipher of Dumuzid, safe and sound. They closed the doors to the King's Suite behind them, leaving Jari tied safely, not to return.

In the lobby, they dropped their bags, Dr. Halifax and Mr. Nero frozen in their tracks.

"Load the truck, Andrew," Brannigan said to his young associate. Outside, a large diesel waited, engine rumbling contentedly.

"My lord," Lily said softly, still unmoving.

Waiting in the lobby were two large, rectangular boxes. *Coffins* some would say. The lids of each were lying on the floor. From their vantage, Lily and Nero could see that each box was half-filled with ice cut in thick square blocks. Beside the truck lay a third coffin, ice rising in a mound from inside.

"These are... for us?" Lily asked, turning wide-eyed to Brick.

"They are indeed," Brannigan said. "Are you all right? You know this is necessary."

She nodded and swallowed, Nero beside her looking just as frightened.

Brannigan took a step towards them and rested one hand on Lily's shoulder and one on Nero's. He pulled them close in a small huddle.

"My friends," he said. "I know you are afraid. I know that you believe yourselves to be walking into the very arms of death. There is nothing I can say to put your fears to rest, nothing accept believe in me. I will not fail you. I will guide you both through this, and together we will share a drink of pomegranate and gin in *Boîte de Nuit du le Fugitif* with an old friend of mine." He smiled at each of them, understanding each of their fears and wanting nothing more than to assuage them.

"Thank you, Brick," Nero said, forcing a smile.

"Yes, thank you, Hugo," Lily said.

Brannigan stared into her eyes. "This is just the beginning, my dear. I promise."

"Professor?" Andrew called, interrupting the group's momentary peace. "The ice is beginning to melt."

"Right you are, Andrew," Brannigan said, finally releasing his brave companions and turning to face the ice-filled coffins, the night, and the peril that waited. "Are we ready, Andrew?"

"Aye, sir. The truck is loaded, and the plane is ready to depart. All that remains..." The young man looked ominously at the large boxes.

Brannigan nodded and reached into his leather satchel. When his hand emerged, it held a pair of long syringes. "It's time," he said.

"Time to die," Nero whispered.

Somberly, Dr. Halifax nodded, praying that when she closed her eyes for the last time, she would–soon enough–open them once again.

Brannigan uncapped two long syringes, and they began.

CHAPTER 20: Lest We Forget, Let's Check Up on One or Two of the Brutal & Bloodthirsty Masterminds Behind the Impending End of the World! (And Allow for the Requisite Time Jump!)

(Time has passed. Days, maybe more. We are in the desert. The sky above is a perfect blue broken only by wisps of cottony clouds.)

A caravan rode in from the north, men on horseback and camelback. They wore robes to cover them from the harsh wind on the Ennedi Plateau. At the head of the group, a tall man with a scimitar hanging from his belt was first off his horse at the sight of water. After the ride through the burning sands, the *Guelta d'Archei* was a most grateful sight.

"*Boire les chevaux*," he shouted to his men. "*Et me faire une boisson*!" With a whip of his robe, he pulled the thin linen wrap away, revealing his face and parched lips.

It was Black Fang Delacroix!

He and a small group of his Legion of Madmen had ridden day and night to arrive here, in the middle of nowhere, at the *Guelta d'Archei* at the command of the Cabal. In the short respites in which Fang slept on the rocky desert ground, he cursed his fate, and he cursed Brick Brannigan.

The expedition to the Temple of Aja had gone so well–
until the very end! *Damn that Brannigan for ruining
everything!* he repeated over and over as he rode. It had
become his mantra. Revenge was more than necessary, he
realized. It was... *inevitable*.

And now, here they stood. His men tended to the
horses as he knelt on the water's edge. He formed a bowl
with his hands and dipped them into the water. It was not
cool, but compared to the burning of the sun it felt like ice,
sending pins and needles into his dry, cracked hands.

"*Mon Dieu*," he said softly. "This is what I get for
crossing the Sahara on horseback."

The *crack* of a gunshot interrupted his complaining.
From a high outcropping of rock, a pair of shearwaters
took flight at the sound. A herd of camels milling about in
the water were unfazed. Fang was not.

He realized all too well what it was. *Someone else has
failed the Cabal*, he thought. *And he has received his
punishment.* He stood upright and gripped the handle of
his scimitar tightly. *Does this await me even now?*

These dark thoughts floated through Delacroix's mind
because he understood better than anyone that his failures
were beginning to mount. Once more, he cursed
Brannigan, and he cursed the choices he'd made that had
brought him here.

Without another thought, he started into the canyon.

The *Guelta d'Archei* was an oasis lost in the heart of
the Sahara Desert. Fang had let his Cabal guide lead him
and his men there, and now having arrived, he was struck
by its beauty. Natural springs met low-lying ground in a
rocky gorge at the *Guelta d'Archei*, bringing the life-
giving water to the surface, forming an unlikely reservoir
in the gorge. Animals and caravans came from far and

wide to bask in the water and drink. Slowly, Fang walked beneath a faded petroglyph painted on the canyon wall as a long, moss-green Nile crocodile glided past him on the water's placid surface. Never before had he seen such a place.

In the dark crevices of the gorge, a white cotton tent shook in the breeze. Outside, two men stood with rifles across their chests.

"*Écarter, les porcs*," he said angrily to the sentries.

Stone-faced, they ignored him.

"I said *move*," he growled.

From within the tent, a deep and gravely voice croaked, "Herr Delacroix, *enter*."

The sentries stepped aside, clearing the entryway. Slowly, Fang stepped inside.

Intricately woven carpets covered the sandy desert ground, and a flickering of lamps lit the dark tent. Some mysterious form of electricity had to be hidden nearby, Fang realized, because a desk was folded into the corner of the tent with a radio crackling on it. Before the set, a giant of a man was huddled in headphones, transcribing some mad messages onto a small pad with a broken pencil.

"Sit, Herr Delacroix," the gravely voice said.

Fang turned to see a tall, carved chair facing him, holding the skeletal shape of an old man in a wilted military uniform. Deep wrinkles lashed his face, and lines of white hair were slicked flat across his bony head. Beside him was a small table covered with documents, some typed, some handwritten.

The old man gestured to a low seat across from his. "Sit," he said.

Fang obliged.

The old man watched Fang's movements, sizing him up, seeming to weigh the value of the master villain across from him.

"You have come very far, very fast," the old man said. "The desert is a harsh place, and that is why I like it. Those who cannot survive the trek to the *Guelta d'Archei* are not worth my time. I would rather they die in the sun on the plateau than waste a bullet of mine, no?" He laughed a lifeless, desiccated laugh, and Fang only watched him, perplexed.

When silence–but for the *buzz* of the radio–had returned to the tent, the old man said, "That large man on the radio, his name is Konig. Do you know what he is writing?"

Fang shook his head slowly.

"He is receiving reports from around the world. We have agents searching for sacred artifacts on each of the seven continents. Many great men are accomplishing remarkable feats on the cliffs of the highest mountains in Switzerland and the deepest caverns of New Zealand. The Earth's secrets are boundless, Herr Delacroix. I do not believe we shall ever turn over a stone and not discover that which should be marveled. And in this world, marvel and wonder are *power*. You understand this, or else you would not have joined the Cabal, no?"

Quiet. Konig continued scribbling in the corner, his pencil never pausing or even slowing. Still, Fang remained silent. Little did he believe it necessary to explain that his joining the Cabal was far from his own decision.

"You have failed us repeatedly, Herr Delacroix."

Fang nodded.

"What have you to say for yourself?"

Fang smiled his black-toothed smile and spread his hands. "I am here, monsieur, to receive what you have to give me. If it be a punishment, let it be swift and merciful. If it be a mere castigation, let it be only swift so that I may return to my duty."

The old man squinted at Fang, an opinion or two perhaps changing. "You are a hard man," he said. "There are those who work with you who believe you to be... what word did he use? *Soulless*. I like that. Yes. What say you to this glorious accusation?"

Fang said nothing to that, and the old man seemed to approve.

"I have men close to you, Herr Delacroix," the old man said. "I would caution you to respect their input when it is given. If you had done so in the past, there is a chance you would not be here now."

Fang was no fool, and the heavy German accent in the old man's voice told him that Von Faust was the inside man. Rather than respond, he simply stared the old man down.

"Your sword," the old man said. "Where did you get it?"

Fang spoke for the first time. "It has belonged to my family for a great many years."

Leaning forward, the old man said, "Damascus steel?"

Fang nodded and the desiccated laugh returned. When it ceased, the old man said, "It is legendary, Damascus steel. Do you believe your sword to be imbued with the same mythological strength of the old Damascus blades?"

Fang did not respond. The old man smiled. "I have no name," the old man said, "I have gone under the cover of

151

an alias for so long that my true name has been forgotten. More years than you could possibly dream, young man. Do you know my alias, the name that was given to me at my rechristening by the Master of the Cabal?"

Fang shook his head.

"They call me... *der Klinge*." The old man smiled. "It means *the Sword*."

Unconsciously, Fang closed his hand around the hilt of his scimitar once more. The old man watched him with his grey eyes but did not speak. The radio *buzzed* on.

Finally, the old man said, "I will not threaten you, Herr Delacroix. Instead, I will give you more men, more guns, more resources. You will find this Brannigan, and you will destroy him. Bring me the Eye of Aja. Also, I have received word that Brannigan now has the Cipher. Seize that, as we believe it to be even more powerful than the Eye. But know this: idle threats do not suit me. One day, inevitably you will fail, and your punishment will be death. It will be neither swift nor merciful, for even now you are earning yourself a fearsome death. When that happens, I will wear your Damascus steel on my belt, do you understand?"

Fang nodded.

"Good. Now leave this place. And when you go, listen for the sound of rifle fire. When you hear it, know that it heralds the death of a man far luckier than you should you fail me again. As I said, you are destined for much worse than a bullet."

With a wave of his hand, Delacroix was dismissed. Silently, he rose. From the corner, Konig the Giant turned and glared at him over his enormous shoulder, a pair of yellow eyes burning with hatred. The monstrous eyes followed Fang each step until he exited into the cool shadows of the gorge once more.

Standing a few paces from the mouth of the tent was Von Faust, hat in hand, a smug grin smeared across his face. With a gloved hand, he wiped sweat from his forehead and readjusted his sinister eyepatch. Fang need not ask how Von Faust had arrived at the *Guelta d'Archei*. Nor need he ask on whose orders had he come.

"Well, Herr Delacroix," Von Faust said. "What did you learn?"

"Enough," Fang said. "I have learned enough." He looked up at the blue sky and sighed. "Are you ready to depart, Monsieur Von Faust?"

Still grinning, Von Faust said, "No. We will stay here tonight and depart in the early morning hours. I want to rest. I want a taste of the women in the camp, for it has been too long. We will leave tomorrow at sun up."

Fang bowed his head and nodded, succumbing to the inevitable shift of power he'd fought for so long, feeling the yoke of his fate settle about his shoulders.

"Yes, Captain," he said.

CHAPTER 21: Welcome to Tangier! Also, Will Our Intrepid Adventurers All Live To See Another Sunrise? Answers (and Scandal) To Follow

Well of *course* Lily and Archibald survive. Good grief.

But it's not that simple. You see, Archibald–resilient bloke that he was–had no trouble reviving from his deep freeze. Brick administered his special rejuvenating cocktail via hypodermic straight to the heart after slight defrosting. Wrapped in blankets, it was only a few short minutes before Nero was coughing and pulling ice crystals from his hair–ahh, the miracle of inexplicable science!

But Lily... well, Lily was saved for last, as Brannigan wanted to clear all distractions from his mind. Her body was removed from ice, the remarkable panacea was administered, and she was wrapped in blankets. Brick waited.

And waited.

On checking his notes, he learned he had never had a body take more than eight minutes to revive completely. Pulse returned at four, normal capillary refill response returned at six, eyes opened at eight.

At eight minutes, Lily's eyes were closed. Her heartbeat–the sound of which Brannigan had dreamt–had not begun again. He began chest compressions–an experimental procedure he'd been pioneering since his days in medical school, applying pressure to her chest in hopes of returning the heart to normal rhythms.

After another full minute, still nothing had happened.

When the ten minute mark passed, Brick administered a second dose of his life-giving elixir and resumed compressions.

At thirteen minutes, he stopped. One final time, he pressed the bell of the stethoscope to her chest and listened.

There was nothing. Dr. Liliana Halifax was dead, and Brick could not bring her back.

Carefully, he lifted her body and held it close. He cursed his failure only because of what it meant for the woman in his arms, never to take another breath again!

Brannigan fancied himself a strong man, a fierce and logical man, but he could not help feeling an overwhelming sadness. He had promised her so much, promised her that it was only the beginning, that he would take care of her, that she had nothing to fear.

And now she was dead.

A solitary tear ran down his cheek–the first time Brick had cried since his brother's funeral eleven years prior–and said, "I am so sorry, Lily. I will miss you dreadfully, and... and we've only just met!"

He sniffled, feeling so sad and perhaps only a little silly. Neither he nor I can help being maudlin at a time like this!

But then... wait! She took a breath!

Brick pulled her slight body away from his great bear-like embrace, his mind snapping back into its scientific mode immediately. He laid her down on the operating table and lifted one eyelid, then the other. Beneath the bright light above, he saw each pupil dilate.

"Hammer of Thor!" he exclaimed.

Moving with all the speed of a cheetah, Brannigan pulled a second blanket around Lily's slowly warming body and lifted her once again. "I need to warm her before it's too late!"

He dashed from the makeshift laboratory through a doorway and up a short flight of steps before exploding through one final door and into the bright North African sun.

The bright and beautiful rays of the sun beat down on them, and Brannigan felt sweat on his face. *Good!* he thought. *Let the sun rain down!*

"Lily," he said softly. "Lily, can you hear me?"

Her breathing had normalized and her eyelids had begun to flutter. "Lily," he said once again.

Slowly, her eyes opened and focused on him.

"Hugo," she said.

She was alive!

He laughed a great and victorious laugh. He felt grateful, more grateful than perhaps he'd ever felt in the whole of his life. "It is so very good to see you, my dear. Welcome back," he smiled. "And... welcome to Tangier!"

***

Lily bathed in one of four small rooms our adventurers shared in the strange building. She could think of nothing more satisfying to do than rinse the feeling of ice (and death) from her body. Perhaps you believe she did not quite understand how close she had come to death, but I can tell you, dear reader, she understood perhaps better than Brannigan himself. In the darkness that was her suspended state, she had experienced long dreams of solitude and loss, and now having awakened, she could not help but think of that great and devilishly handsome man, that *Brick Brannigan*. It was not only that he'd saved her life. No. There was something else... something she could not put her finger on. She tried to think empirically, but truly, it was difficult!

When she was finished, she dressed in her own clothes–cleaned and pressed since being moved from Nigeria (and feeling quite alien after her slumber)–and returned to the roof.

Brannigan sat on the concrete ledge of the building, legs dangling, watching the water of the Strait of Gibraltar. A triple-masted schooner silently glided across the Strait as seagulls cawed overhead. From her vantage, Lily could see that Brannigan was smiling like a dope.

"Hugo," she said softly as she approached, feeling a delightful flutter in her chest.

Quickly he turned, his smile not ebbing even for a moment. If anything, it grew at the sight of her. "Hello, Lily," he said. "How are you feeling?"

He moved to stand before she gestured him to sit once more. She paused a foot or so from him. "You're... sitting on the edge?" she asked.

He nodded. "It's perfectly safe, my dear." He extended a hand to her.

She gave it a thought, pausing only momentarily before taking his hand and sitting beside him. "You know," she said, "I used to be terrified by heights. And only a... well, a short while ago, I dashed across rooftops in Nigeria in pursuit of an international criminal."

"You did indeed," Brannigan said. "You saved my life, you know."

"And you mine!"

They smiled at each other, feeling the mutual awkwardness that arises when awkward people are placed in romantic situations–only exacerbated by the preponderance of near-death experiences!

After a long pause, they both spoke at once:

Lily said, "When I was dead–" and Brannigan said, "I have to tell you–"

But they both stopped.

"What?" Lily asked.

"Eh, no, you first," Brannigan said, blushing.

Lily said, "Umm," and then lapsed into silence.

You see, this is what I mean about awkward people in romantic situations.

Lily looked at the rakishly handsome man beside her, wanting nothing more than to kiss him. Her own self-doubt, however–even in the face of her *carpe diem-you-were-just-dead-and-so-you-should-never-wait* mentality–won out. She changed the subject.

Little did she know, Brannigan was having the exact same thoughts! He looked at the beautiful woman beside him, and despite what he wanted more than words could express, he fathomed no way that a woman such as Liliana Halifax could ever desire a man such as himself.

What a pair of nitwits!

"So this is Tangier?" Lily asked as nonchalantly as possible.

"Yes, it is," Brannigan replied–also as nonchalantly as

possible. "It's technically called the Tangier International Zone because it's truly an international city." Brannigan said, realizing but unable to halt his awkward eruption of facts as they spewed from his mouth. "It's a remarkable city for a great many reasons, but the presence of French, Spanish, British, Portuguese, Italian, Belgian, Dutch... ummm... Swedish and American citizens make it truly one of a kind."

Lily swallowed and tried to think of a very intelligent question.

"This is... the ocean?" she asked, realizing too late that her chosen question was not, in fact, intelligent at all.

"Uh, well, it's the Strait of Gibraltar actually–"

"Yes, of course," she said, shaking her head. "That was silly," she muttered.

"No, no not at all," Brick said. "You know, the delineation between the Strait and the Mediterranean was always a bit fuzzy for me to determine, as well. I've been puzzled by that once or twice."

"You've been to Tangier many times?"

Brannigan nodded. "Yes. In my much younger and much wilder days, I helped battle the last of the Barbary pirates on these waters, negotiating ransoms and even kidnapping a few pirates of my own to exchange for hostages. Tangier, Tunis, Tripoli, Algiers, Alexandria, Carthage, Rabat, and Casablanca–among others–are wondrous cities. The medina in Tangier is particularly–"

"I'm sorry, the medina?"

"It's the old quarter. Many of these cities are being modernized," he said the word as if it tasted terrible, "and changed, expanded and rebuilt. The medina is where you find the history."

"Is that where we are now?"

"We are indeed," he said. "We are on the roof of *Le Boîte de Nuit du le Fugitif*, owned by a woman for whom I once performed a favor."

"*Le Boîte de Nuit du le Fugitif*?" Lily asked. "'The Nightclub of... the Fugitive'?"

Brannigan laughed. "It's a rather dramatic name, although in Tangier it's just called *le Fugitif*. Such dramatics are to be expected from a Frenchmen," he said.

"Or French*woman*," Lily corrected.

"True, true."

Silence again. Awkward, so more of the same. Each of our adventurers wanted nothing more than to fill it, yet neither seemed blessed with the capacity. Ah, damn that niggling self-doubt!

"I can... um, show you around?" Brannigan finally ventured as a foghorn blew on the strait, signaling the arrival of a ferry from Andalusia. "If you like...?" he said, after a long pause.

Lily turned to Brick and kissed him. Yes! There is that adventuress blood that flows through her veins! Perhaps her *carpe diem* mentality did not go to waste after all!

Brannigan blushed, some strange part of him thinking (just for the smallest fraction of a second) that Lily's brazenness was rather scandalous. Thankfully, that minuscule part was stampeded by the rest of his brain as it said, "*You know, I really do quite like this Lily Halifax.*" There is, after all, something to be said for a bold and declarative woman. And why would an adventurer ever want anything less than an adventuress? (And vice versa.)

The kiss lasted for quite some time, dear reader, though we will not go into detail, as even adventurers deserve their extraordinary moments to be experienced in peace.

When it was finished, Lily said, "Show me *Le Boîte de Nuit du le Fugitif*, Hugo Brannigan. Show me Tangier. Show me *everything*!"

CHAPTER 22: The Toast of *Le Boîte de Nuit du le Fugitif*, and Another Max at the Offices of the American Legation of Tangier (Always Willing, Unfortunately Not Always So Able!)

Brannigan led Lily downstairs, a crooked wooden flight of steps that curved as if it had itself lost its way. Passing their suite of rooms that she'd only just discovered, he continued down to the ground floor and main space of *Le Boîte de Nuit du le Fugitif*, his hand resting on the small of her back all the while. It was a feeling he relished as much as she did.

The Fugitive was closed, admittedly taking something away from the nocturnal atmosphere. A bandstand overlooked a broad dance floor to the left of the stairwell landing and a long black bar ran the length of the opposite wall, a collage of bottles peppering the wall behind the bar–empty save for the seated Mr. Nero and a solitary figure tending. Between the bar and dance floor were twenty or so small round cocktail tables.

"Here, here, and here," Nero was saying. He wore a thin cotton shirt, still wet from his defrosting, and was pulling the neck of the shirt low to expose scars on his chest.

"Pistol shots, you say?" the bartender asked in a thickly accented voice. From where Lily stood, she could not make out the young woman's face. She wore all black clothing and had raven black hair obscuring her face.

"Not a pistol, it was a rifle!" Nero exclaimed. "A . 30-.30 Winchester. You take three slugs from one of those and no Doctor on this Earth will do anything but kiss you up to God."

"But not you, Monsieur," the barkeep said.

"No, not me, Miette," Nero smiled broadly and knocked back his drink. The entrance of Brannigan and Lily caught his eye and the pilot turned, grinning. "Liliana!" he said, rising.

He crossed the space and hugged her. He felt feverishly warm, but his joy was evident, only buoyed by the rich smell of alcohol on his breath. "I am so glad to see you on your feet again!" He smiled, and Lily noted just the slight slur in his speech.

"Archibald," she said, not unkindly. "It is good to see you, as well. Quite the trip we had, wasn't it?"

"From Port Harcourt to Tangier?" He smiled. "I've never travelled such a great distance so quickly! Just like *that*!" He snapped his fingers and laughed. "That Brick must be a better pilot than I imagined."

"I had a good teacher," Brannigan said sheepishly.

"Pish posh," Nero dismissed him. "You're speaking of the trip to Delhi when I was shot and you were forced to fly? You've come a long way since then, I say!"

Brannigan smiled. "Lily," he said, "This is Mignonette Tati, an old friend."

Crossing the space, Lily shook hands with the quiet Frenchwoman behind the bar. Dressed all in black–and remarkably beautiful–the short woman was quite mysterious indeed. Long bangs covered one eye, but she smiled easily, her crimson lipsticked lips showing nothing but kindness, if withdrawn kindness.

"Welcome to *Le Boîte de Nuit du le Fugitif*, mon amie. Any friend of Hugo's is a friend of mine," she shook Lily's hand gently, her grip delicate but strong. "And please, call me Miette."

"And you can call me Lily. Thank you so much for welcoming us. I believe in no small measure, we owe you our lives."

Miette shook her head. "Hugo is, how you say, resilient. A very resilient man. If he could not find help here in *le Fugitif*, he would find it elsewhere. With him, your lives are always safe."

Lily looked at the man beside her, still feeling his hand on the small of her back. "I'm learning that very quickly," she said.

Miette looked from Lily up to Brannigan knowingly and smiled. "A toast then? I insist." She disappeared behind the bar momentarily before returning with four clean glasses. She turned and lifted a bottle. "This is new," she said. "But it is good, very good. It's called *pastis*."

She poured four small glasses of the milky yellow liquid and passed them out.

"*A vote santé*," she said with a reclusive smile. "My new friends."

As one, the four threw back their drinks.

Nero slammed his empty glass back on the counter and sighed, Miette lowered hers to the sink to rinse it, Lily shook her head and made a pained face, and Brannigan only smiled.

Watching him closely, Miette said, "What are your

164

plans now, Hugo?"

Brannigan returned his and Lily's glasses to the bar where Miette took them to wash. "The poison has been cured–thanks to you," he said.

"And Monsieur *Le Duc*," Miette added.

"Yes, and Monsieur *Le Duc*. My friends are both alive. We've shared our official welcome-to-Tangier toast," he nodded as if checking items off a list.

"Yes, and?"

"And soon we will depart."

"What?" Nero said, eyes wide. "But we've only just arrived!"

"As a matter of fact, Arch, you've been in Tangier for six days," Brannigan said. "It took me that long to get the necessary materials to cure your poisoning."

"But we've only just woken," Nero said, turning his predatory gaze to Miette. "There is so much I'd like to see and do!"

"*Vous n'avez aucune chance,* mon ami," Miette said laughing. "*Vous n'êtes pas mon type.*"

Lily tried to stifle a laugh and failed. She raised a hand to block her mouth. Thankfully, Nero did not notice, so lost was he in Miette's deep, dark eyes.

"I love when you speak in French," he said. "It is so... very romantic."

"*Vous me dégoûtent, cochon,*" Miette said seductively. "*Je préfère baiser un baudet.*"

Lilly and Brannigan merely shook their heads as Nero continued his useless attempts at wooing Mademoiselle Tati.

"Come with me, Lily," Brannigan said. "We've things

to do, people to see."

Together, they left Nero in the more-than-capable hands of Miette as they opened the front doors and returned to the Moroccan sunshine.

Down a step and our two adventurers stood in the southern end of Tangier's medina. Street vendors filled every alcove. Overhead, canvas and linen canopies cast shadows across stalls filled with ceramic tagines, olives, silver jewelry, pomegranates, fresh meats, lemons, and things Lily could not begin to describe. Her senses were overwhelmed. People rushed past, a river moving up and down the street. A pair of Spanish lovers were arguing in a stall over the price of almonds as a young Brit strolled past, talking up a young girl and pushing a red bicycle. The smell of saffron, tahini, and tobacco filled the air.

"This is extraordinary," she said softly.

Brannigan smiled. "And we've only just stepped outside, my dear."

Gently, he guided her up the street–*Rue du Four*, he said–towards a crowded intersection where businessmen haggled over the price of a goat.

"Where are we going?" Lily asked, her voice rising to be heard over the din of the street market.

"The American Legation," Brannigan said, also forced to raise his voice. "To meet a friend!"

"The American what?"

"Legation. It holds the American Consulate," Brannigan said. "I've a friend there who may be able to answer our questions."

The pair continued, winding their way through crowded streets as the market was replaced with residential home fronts stacked on top of the next in the narrow streets. As the crowd thinned, Lily leaned close to Brannigan and spoke once again.

"What's next for us, Hugo?" Once more, his hand had found the small of her back, and the feeling of it made her smile.

"After the consulate, we will arrange for some transportation back to America. I do not like possessing such highly prized artifacts so far from home."

"Home already?" she asked. "If we are to return to Branford University, why was I sent here with the disc? Why did Dr. Max not simply wait for you to return?"

Brannigan stroked his not-insubstantial facial hair. "That is a good question, my dear. If we had the scroll I just sent to him, it would not be so urgent that we return. Why do you think Quincy sent you?"

"Dr. Max must have believed there was some purpose in my bringing the Cipher to you. Perhaps he believed that together we could decipher it. Have you examined it?"

"But without the scroll? And no, I've not had a chance–"

"Shouldn't we do that before returning home? Let's not worry about the scroll just yet," she said, a glint in her eye.

Brannigan thought for a moment as they turned another corner. "Perhaps," he said. "It's just... the Eye of Aja worries me."

"Eye of Aja?" So much had happened since she had spoken with Quincy Max back at Branford that she could not seem to sort out her thoughts. "Remind me?" she asked.

Brannigan smiled. "It was why I was in Nigeria, my dear. It was what took me into the depths of the jungle.

You must remember, Quincy sent me to Nigeria first on what he described as 'the opening salvo in a war that would last for centuries.' And I thought I had a penchant for theatrics."

"You know, Hugo, he did explain much to me about the Cabal's intentions."

"Don't you mean *intention*, dear? As in a singular intention? I believe there is only one thing they want."

"Yes, Hugo, unfortunately you are right about that. Ending the world?"

"Yes, dear. I am not sure why anyone would want that, but there you have it."

Lily sighed. "Yes. You know, not to change the subject, but why don't you let me have a look at the Cipher? You know Dr. Max sent me because of my research."

"Did he now?"

"Yes. He believed I would be quite helpful to the cause."

Brannigan smiled. "I believe you already have been. And the fight has just begun, my dear. Ah," he stopped and pointed. "There it is."

***

The American Legation was a white stuccoed stone building near the southernmost edge of the medina. Judging by the collection of languages they heard as they entered–French, Spanish, Arabic, English, and German– the courtyard was crowded with men and women from all around the world. Brannigan guided Lily past a small bubbling fountain and up a flight of steps towards the private offices.

"Let's hope Mortimer is in," he said.

"Mortimer?"

Brannigan smiled. "You'll see."

At the end of the balcony overlooking the courtyard was an open door. Brannigan led Lily to it and knocked on the jamb. From the dark confines inside, a weary old voice said, "Yes?" Brick led Lily into the office.

The room was dark compared to the glaring sunlight outside, and Lily's and Brick's eyes had to adjust before they could see anything.

The office was more akin to a library. Dark wooden shelves and furniture filled the room, heavy furniture imported from America. Heavy hardback tomes filled the shelves and a dozen or so were stacked precariously on the broad desk at the back of the small room. But for the sunlight pouring in from the open door, the only other light was a small green-shaded lamp on the desk.

"Can I help you?" the old voice asked.

"Mortimer?" Brick ventured.

"Yes. And you are..."

"It's me, Brick Brannigan!"

The old man laughed, joy filling his voice for the first time. "Brick!" he said. "I'm delighted to see you, my friend! It's been too long!" From behind the pile of books on the desk, an ancient man rose, a bushy white beard hanging down to his mid-chest. His likeness to Quincy Max was astounding.

"Uh, Mortimer," Brick said slowly, "we spoke yesterday, remember?"

"We did? Ah... yes, perhaps we did," the old man said, scratching his head. "I remember your friend, though. She's lovely. You dog, you!"

"My name is Lily," Dr. Halifax said, reaching out to shake the old man's hand.

"Oh sure, sure!" he said, shaking her hand heartily.

Brannigan said, "She is a beauty, isn't she? Unfortunately, Mortimer, this isn't just a social call. I'm checking up on something I needed your help with, do you remember?"

"Help," the old man said. "Help, hmmm. Well, no, I don't remember. Why not give me a, uh, reminder?"

"Have a seat, my dear," Brannigan said to Lily with a smile. "This could take a minute."

And take a minute it did. As a matter of fact, it took nearly 60 to find the requisite paperwork and handwritten notes on old Mortimer's desk and another twenty to go over them with the old timer before Mortimer had been brought back up to speed.

"Let me make a call," Mortimer said, excusing himself momentarily to use the telephone.

Brannigan took a seat beside Lily and ran his hand along her bare arm. "Hopefully," he said, "we'll be getting some good news shortly."

Lily smiled and leaned in close to Brick. "What exactly is going on, Hugo?"

"Well, you probably know by now based on simple deduction, but Mortimer is Quincy's brother. Mortimer Max is older by I believe two years. The Max family is quite large. I've been running into brothers and sisters of old Q's for years. They're everywhere."

"I was beginning to suspect," Lily said. "He's a dead

ringer!"

"He is, indeed."

"And why are we here?"

"So you remember when Archibald said I was not much of a pilot?"

"Yes."

"Well, I'm not. I sort of... *crashed* the plane when I landed at the Tangier airfield."

"You crashed the *Belladonna*? Oh Hugo!"

"It's all right, Lily. All's well that ends well, isn't it? Unfortunately, not for Archibald's plane."

"Is it...?"

"Destroyed? No, but it needed substantial repair."

"So you came to Mortimer?"

Brannigan nodded. "Mortimer Max has the money and connections to do large-scale mechanical repairs. If I thought Miette would know someone, I would have gone through her, but this was a Curtiss C-46 Commando, not exactly a busted tricycle. I needed someone with army connections."

"And so you came to Mortimer."

"Exactly. The only problem is..."

"...he's not exactly–"

The door to the back office opened, cutting Lily off. Our adventurers looked up and smiled at the old man.

"Brick!" he said. "I'm delighted to see you, my friend! It's been too long!"

Brannigan sighed. "Yes, it has, Mortimer. Were you just on the phone?"

"Um, I'm sorry?"

"Were you just using the phone in the back office?"

"Why, yes, yes I was!"

"And what did you learn?"

"Learn? Well, a plane I'm having repaired should be ready first thing in the morning."

"Oh, that's splendid," Brannigan said.

"So what brings you here, Brick?" Mortimer asked.

"Just to get some input from you about a Cipher we have. It's called the Cipher of Dumuzid."

"A what? Who?"

Brannigan wilted, ever so slightly. "A Cipher, Mortimer. It's a... a rare archaeological relic."

Mortimer waved a hand dismissively. "You need to ask Quincy about that," he said. "He's the one who knows about that stuff."

Brannigan nodded. "Fine, fine," he said. "Do you have any books on Sumer?"

The old man played unconsciously with his beard. "Sumer," he said. "Sumer. Hmmm. Why, I think so, yes." He trundled to the bookshelf and, without pause, picked a thin blue volume off the shelf and handed it to Brick. "Here, my friend. Take this. I hope it helps in whatever you're working on!"

"Thank you, Mortimer," Brick said, rising. He shook the old man's hand. Lily was one step behind.

"Thank you, Mr. Max. It was a pleasure to, uh, see you again."

"Yes, it was! It certainly was. You take good care of Brick, now. He gets himself into such trouble!"

Lily smiled. "He certainly does, doesn't he?" The old man nodded animatedly and Lily laughed. "I'll do what I can."

"Thank you!" Mortimer said. "And please, stop by again! It's so nice to see you both. Take care now!"

Brannigan pulled the office door shut behind him.

"What a delightful man," Lily said.

"He is, yes. I wish you could have met him a few years ago. He was just like Quincy, Lily. Bright-eyed, sharp, quick-witted, and fierce. I asked him about the Cipher because he was once as formidable an archaeological mind as Quincy himself, maybe more. Unfortunately, the years have been hard on him."

"You hoped the name would call to mind some recognition?"

Brannigan nodded and passed Lily the small blue volume. "It seems the only thing he remembers anymore are his books. He goes through them day and night, arranging and cataloguing them. I don't know if that book will be of any help, but it was worth a shot."

Lily paged through the small volume as they crossed the balcony towards the stairs leading down to the courtyard.

"I'm well-enough versed in the Sumerian cuneiform, but I'll need all the help I can get if we hope to make progress on the Cipher."

"We'll be hopeful," Brannigan said. "You never know what this small text could contain."

"I have hope, Hugo," Lily said. "Together, I believe we can crack the Cipher of Dumuzid!"

Now, call it stars in their eyes or what have you, but something about that sunny Moroccan afternoon made our adventurers careless, and neither noticed the bearded gent follow them across the courtyard.

Little did they know he carried a revolver in his pocket... and murder in his heart!

CHAPTER 23: Blood in the Streets & Bullets in the Bath House

Now, you may be wondering "What the hell are they doing speaking so injudiciously about this incredibly rare and maybe priceless artifact wanted by an international secret society/doomsday cult?? Careless?"

In truth, I was wondering the same thing myself.

"From what I remember," Lily said, "the cuneiforms on the disc were certainly Sumerian, but it wasn't that simple."

"Ellis said that this Cipher would transcend everything we'd expected of it, especially when used in conjunction with the scroll I discovered," Brannigan said, stopping at a street vendor to buy stuffed dates. "Care for one?" he asked.

Lily tried one and was delighted. "Ellis?" she asked. "Remind me?"

"Ellis Spooner, he's also a Professor at–"

"Ah, Dr. Spooner," Lily said, skeptically.

"So I see his reputation has suffered further at the hands of the more lecture-oriented faculty?" Brannigan asked with a smile.

"He is..." Lily chose her words carefully. "Not well-loved."

Brannigan shook his head and raised a date to his

mouth. "A shame. The man–"

A bullet *SNIPPP*ed the date from his hand in a flurry of cinnamon, almonds, and ground walnuts.

"Sword of Damocles!" Brannigan exclaimed, pulling Lily behind a stuccoed hostel for cover. "We have been careless!"

Why, yes Brick, you have been careless indeed!

Although, in truth, Drs. Brannigan and Halifax– unacquainted with the Cabal as they were–could not even begin to understand the far reaching grasp of the terrible organization. Their agents are *everywhere* (e.g. the American Legation's janitor, the young Brit pushing the red bicycle, the man playing the tbilat on the corner of *Rue Khath* and *Rue al Ferran*, etc, etc). Had Drs. Brannigan and Halifax wanted to maintain the secret of the Cipher, they would have needed to avoid the Tangier International Zone altogether (hotbed of spies that it was!).

Brannigan took Lily by the hand and pulled her down a narrow alleyway as bullets zipped overhead. A commotion had started on the street behind them and Brick could hear shouting in Arabic and French accompanied by further gunshots and the revving of a motorcycle engine.

"Here!" he said, pulling Lily through an open door that led them into the filthy back kitchen of a street cafe. "Excuse me, excuse me," Brannigan said as he slipped past chefs and waiters, overturning stacks of plates and pots, all the while being scolded in Arabic. He spared one glance behind him to see pistol-waving mad villains rush into the kitchen. "Faster, Lily!" he shouted.

"Deepest apologies!" Lily said as they pushed through a bead curtain and raced through a crowded dining room. Patrons looked up, surprised, at the sound of shouting. Bullets hummed overhead like angry bees.

Together, Brannigan and Halifax pushed open the front doors and reentered the flowing crowd of the medina, back in the heart of the street market.

"I was foolish," Brannigan said as he pushed past a group of American expatriates. "Tangier is not the sort of city where you speak idly!"

"What do you mean? Are we safe–"

A bullet ripped through a bushel of endive a local vendor peddled, raising a few screams as Brick ducked and said, "Not yet!"

Behind them, their pursuers were splitting up, the masked evildoers disappearing into the crowd, their fervor not diminished one bit. Our two adventurers turned a sharp corner and slammed into the hairy midriff of a camel, chewing cud in front of a produce market.

"Excuse me!" Brannigan shouted as he pushed past the huge mammal and turned another corner. "We need to get back to *le Fugitif*," he said. "We need help!"

The new street brought only new troubles. That awful roar of a motorcycle engine returned, approaching from the far end of the street as the shouting of voices rose.

"Not this way, Hugo!" Lily said. "We need to go the other way!"

"But–"

A bullet slammed into the masonry above Brannigan's head. He shook his head. "No, you're right! The other way!"

Lily took Brannigan's hand and pulled him in the opposite direction, heading deeper into the medina, the streets growing darker, narrower, more twisted, and more crowded. With each corner they turned, the sound of the revving motorcycle diminished, but the continued *PAP*

PAP PAP of small arms fire was unending.

When finally the gunfire stopped, Brannigan breathlessly pulled Lily into the dank lobby of a hotel.

"What are you doing?" she asked. "We need to keep–"

"Wait, my dear," Brannigan said. "First we need help. Then we can keep moving."

"Help?"

"Aye, help!"

The two rushed to the counter where an overweight bearded man in a fez smoked a pipe drowsily.

"Good afternoon, sir!" Brick said, trying to catch his breath. "I wonder, could we–"

A stream of Arabic rushed from the man's mouth.

"Damnit," Brannigan said. "I have not quite... eh... mastered Arabic," he admitted sheepishly. Turning to Lily, he said, "Doctor?"

Lily blushed. "I'm more of the dead languages type. Sumerian, Latin, Akkadian–"

Turning back to the man at the desk, the Professor said, "*Français? Russkjj? Español?*" Brannigan rattled through the languages in which he was apparently fluid, accent perfect for each.

"*Un peu Français,*" the large man finally said.

"*Ah, bon!*" Brannigan smiled. "*Puis-je utiliser votre téléphone?*"

"*Quoi?*" the man said.

"*Votre téléphone,*" Brannigan said, raising a hand to his ear and pantomiming a telephone. "*Téléphone.*"

"*Pour un coût,*" the man smiled smugly.

Brannigan muttered some unmentionable phrases that

made Lily blush as he pulled a wad of money from his pocket. He handed the man a few notes that were counted very slowly.

"*Nous sommes pressés, monsieur!*" Brannigan said angrily.

When the man was happy with what he'd been paid, he pulled a heavy black phone from beneath the counter and set it on an open newspaper.

"*Merci,*" Brannigan said with a frown.

One finger worked the rotary as he held the handset to his ear. He turned to Lily and said, "Keep an eye on the street, darling. We need to be ready to move at a moment's notice."

Lily nodded and turned, watching the street but not leaving Brannigan's side. In the shadowy medina street, only disinterested pedestrians flowed past.

"*Oui?*" a voice crackled through the handset.

"Miette," Brannigan said, relieved. "We're in... a spot of trouble."

"*Où êtes-vous?*" she asked.

"We're in a hotel on..." he turned to the proprietor. "*Où sommes-nous?*" he asked.

"117 *Rue Kadiria,*" the fat man said as he chewed his pipe stem. "*Le Fleur du Désert Hôtel.*"

Brannigan repeated the address and waited. Lily watched as he received some instructions. Shouting outside made it impossible for her to hear Miette's soft voice.

"Hugo, I think we need to move," she said quietly.

"Thank you, Miette," Brannigan said. "We will be there." He hung up the phone. "*Merci, mon ami,*"

Brannigan said to the man at the desk before turning away.

"Well?" Lily asked.

"She's coming, and she's bringing help."

"We wait here? That seems... unwise."

"No, my dear," Brannigan said, wiping sweat from his brow. "She's meeting us somewhere else."

"Where?"

He smiled. "The *Hammam*."

***

Ahhh, what North African expedition would be complete without a trip to a *Hammam*? Brannigan tried to explain what it was on the short walk to the local *Hammam*, but cautionary silence cut his exposition short– wary as they were of pursuit. And so, dear reader, our exposition will be cut short as well.

Brannigan paid for them both at the door, and together they slipped inside the large stone building.

A *Hammam*, put succinctly, is a steam bath not completely dissimilar to a Turkish steam bath. The building was large and ornate inside, marble columns holding the high dome of the main room. Inside, the light was dim and steam filled each room in dense clouds.

At that time of the late afternoon, the *Hammam* was surprisingly empty, and Brannigan led Lily inside, passing only a handful of disinterested patrons.

"Where are we?"

"*Shhh*," he said with a smile. "We've not taken our shoes off, do you want to get us kicked out?"

Fully dressed, our adventurers snuck deeper into the

grand structure, finally coming to a rest in a back room where they took a seat on long stone benches, wet with humidity. Candles set at periodic intervals around the room flickered, struggling to stay lit, casting small orbs of light around the long, narrow room.

"Are you all right?" he asked softly.

Lily nodded, wiping strands of wet hair from her face. "Are you?"

He nodded. "I'm hungry."

Lily stifled a laugh and agreed.

Looking into her eyes, Brannigan could not help but kiss her–danger be damned! Unfortunately, their steamy moment (get it?) was interrupted by the heavy sound of boots on tile. Brannigan pulled away, eyes narrowing in concentration.

The muted sound of mumbled Arabic could be heard through the empty rooms.

"They're here," he said. "How did they find us so quickly?"

He stood and led Lily to the back of the room, the darkest corner. Sweat ran down his face in beads as he reached the back wall. Feeling around on the stone wall, he cursed under his breath.

"There is no rear exit to this room," he said. "My memory said otherwise."

Lily swallowed. "So you're saying..."

"We're trapped," he said.

A *click* of metal sounded at the opposite end of the long room. Brannigan turned and stepped in front of Lily. Slowly, candles began to die, extinguishing in a terribly convenient line moving away from the door. In the otherwise poorly lit room, obscured by clouds of steam as it was, our adventurers could discern very little.

Slowly, Brannigan inched forward, listening and waiting. From a distance, he could hear angry voices and a number of footsteps splashing through water.

"*Er muss hier sein,*" a German voice said. "*Finden Sie ihn*! *Tötet ihn!*"

"Nazis," Brannigan whispered. From his belt, he slipped a coffin handled Bowie knife from its sheath.

From behind him, Lily whispered, "Hugo? Hu–"

He raised a hand to interrupt her. Someone was in the room. In the darkness there was no way of telling if it was one man or three. A raspy breath sounded in the mist. Moments later, a boot squeaked on the tile.

Brannigan lunged into the steam like an attacking lion, seizing on the faint silhouette of an armed soldier. Lily took a few steps forward and froze at the sight of Brannigan wrestling the young man's rifle away from him, one hand locked over the trigger guard, struggling to stifle a shot. Lily raced to his aid, aware that if the gun should fire, the soldiers would come down on them like an avalanche.

"Lily," Brannigan said. "Get... back!"

Ignoring his warnings, she lashed out, kicking her heavy boot and connecting with the young soldier's temple. Under Brannigan's weight, the soldier went limp.

"Oh," Brannigan said, taking a deep breath. "Or you can... do that!"

"I'm not so helpless you know, Hugo," Lily said with a smile.

"I know, darling. I'm sorry. Thank you for your–"

Gunfire lanced through the silence of the *Hammam* like thunder. Together, Brannigan and Lily ducked and raced through the room's exit, sprinting into the *Hammam*'s main room.

Balustrades broke up the space, running between the pillars of the tiered floor. Our adventurers raced from one pillar to the next, avoiding gunshots as best they could as the interior marble walls were shredded by errant bullets. Shouting voices rang throughout the room, echoing off the wet walls.

At this point, Lily and Brannigan were both soaked to the skin, but their spirits were not deterred. "We need to make a run for it, Lily," he said softly. Another hail of gunfire was met with screams and shouts of pain, making Brannigan grimace. "This could be very bad."

Peeking out from behind a pillar, Brannigan watched as a squad of Nazi soldiers was mowed down by an unseen assailant.

"Oh, wait," he said. "Perhaps not."

A fierce screeching voice cut through the echoes of gunfire and the sound of running water, sending a few last German soldiers scattering for their lives. A monstrous roar of gunfire ended their mad dash.

"Wait." Lily looked up. "That voice... was that?"

Brannigan smiled. "I think it was."

Silence fell over the *Hammam*. Only the sound of running water could be heard. Brannigan and Lily waited, perhaps for some signal.

A clatter of a gun reloading was the first signal. The second was a soft and gentle voice–a far cry from the bellicose howl they'd heard only moments earlier–saying, "Hugo? *Êtes-vous vivant*? *Professeur* Halifax? *Êtes-vous vivant? Pouvez-vous m'entendre, mes amis?*"

Brannigan laughed. "We are alive, Miette."

From the mist, the slight Frenchwoman emerged, still dressed head to toe in black, red lipstick perfect. In her arms were a pair of .45 Thompson submachine guns.

Brannigan rose to his full height, a belly laugh escaping his lips. "Still using two Tommies?" he asked, nodding at her choice of weapon.

The small woman shrugged. "*Ils font le travail,*" she said with a mischievous grin.

Brannigan laughed again. "Is Nero with you?"

She shook her head. "He needed rest. But I can handle alone," she said. "I do not worry, Hugo."

Lily stepped out from behind a pillar, pulling her wet hair back. "With two machine guns, I wouldn't worry either," she said.

Miette smiled. "*Allons-y!*" she said. "I am hungry. And this steam makes my hair curl."

CHAPTER 24: The Belle Hops, The Cipher of Dumuzid, The Black-Toothed Cur, and The Sickness!

On returning to *Le Boîte de Nuit du le Fugitif*, our adventurers (five now including Andrew–he had spent the day in the Garrison Library in Gibraltar) broke bread. Miette's in-house chef put together an early dinner of couscous and a cold taktouka salad. To drink our travelers shared green tea with mint as well as brandy.

"*Bon appétit*," Miette said, finally taking a seat at a table just off *le Fugitif*'s dance floor. As the couscous was passed around the table, she asked, "What did you discover today, Hugo? Prior to your afternoon adventure, that is."

"Adventure?" Nero asked as he received the couscous from Andrew. He looked down at the dish and frowned. After a moment he passed it to Lily without taking any.

"We had a spot of trouble this afternoon on returning from the American Legation," Brannigan explained. "Thankfully, Miette was able to assist us." He looked at Nero. "Are you all right, Arch? You look pale. And you're not eating."

Nero forced a smile. "Upset stomach, old chap. Nothing to worry. Something must not have agreed with me. Anyway, what did you discover at the American Legation?"

"We received a reference text on the Sumerian cuneiform from Mr. Max," Lily said, taking a sip of tea.

"Max?" Nero said. Despite his pallor, he smiled. "Which one?"

"Mortimer," Brannigan said. Turning to Miette, he asked, "How is the book, by the way?"

"It is drying beside the fire, as you say. It should be done soon."

"Wonderful. Thank you."

The Frenchwoman nodded once and took a bite of her taktouka. "And your... eh. Craft? How you say? *Avion*?"

"Plane," Brannigan said.

"Yes, of course. Your plane?"

"It will be ready to fly in the morning."

"Why wouldn't it?" Nero asked suspiciously.

"No reason," Brannigan and Lily said simultaneously.

"Just getting fueled up!" Andrew said. "And... um, washed! Everything is fine."

Nero raised a glass of tea to take a sip when his hand began shaking and he dropped his glass, spilling the tea across the table.

"Archibald!" Lily said. "Are you all right?"

"You look terrible, my friend," Brannigan added.

"I feel... ugh. Not well, I confess. Perhaps I should lay down. Please excuse me, friends." Slowly, he rose on unsteady legs. Brannigan rose with him and together the two climbed the stairs for the visitor's rooms.

Lily, Andrew, and Miette ate in silence. When Brannigan returned a few minutes later, he looked concerned.

"Is he all right, Hugo?" Lily asked.

"I believe he is. Whatever he has came on quite suddenly, didn't it?"

"Has it anything to do with your, eh, *médecine étrange*?"

"*Médecine étrange*? Oh you mean when I revived him?" he shook his head. "You're feeling all right, aren't you dear?" he asked Lily.

Dr. Halifax nodded as she chewed her couscous. When she swallowed she said, "I feel perfectly fine. Is there a chance it's a simple bug?"

Brannigan only shook his head. "I fear there are rarely simple bugs in stories such as this."

***

After dinner, Miette excused herself. The club would be opening shortly and she needed to prepare the bar. A member of the waitstaff cleared the dishes while Brannigan, Lily, and Andrew adjourned to a table in the corner where they began to examine the Cipher of Dumuzid in earnest.

"Where did this come from, Professor?" young Caine asked curiously.

"I brought it," Lily said. "It was sent to Branford by Dr. Spooner."

"Ellis found it?" Andrew smiled. "I knew he would!"

"As did he, my boy," Brannigan nodded. "As did he."

"How long had he searched for this?" Lily asked.

Brick looked at her and smiled. "Nearly six years, my dear."

"Good lord."

"Now... let's see what we can see."

Slowly, he unwrapped the leather binding around the disc and laid it out on the tabletop beneath a halo of light shining down from the ceiling. The black disc was about seven inches in diameter and was covered in hieroglyphic-like symbols. Brannigan was familiar with Egyptian hieroglyphics and Arabic characters, but these were completely different.

"You said these are... what, Lily?"

"Cuneiforms," she said. "It's most certainly Sumerian in origin."

"But it doesn't look to be quite that old," Andrew said.

"That's right, Andrew, and that's what made me so confused when I first saw it."

Brannigan turned to his young associate. "What does this remind you of, my boy?" When his partner only shook his head, the Professor continued. "The Temple of Aja, of course!"

"I don't understand, Professor," Andrew said.

"Remember, my boy, that the construction of the Temple was almost Roman in its architecture? And we haven't even mentioned the Clockwork Man. Both seemed remarkably anachronistic for an ancient Temple on the Niger Delta?"

"A fair point, sir," young Caine nodded.

"And this is very much the same," Brannigan said pointing. "Can you pinpoint *when* this was made, Lily?"

She shook her head. "Not without more tools. Do you have your chemistry kit, Hugo? Or your microscope?"

"They were both damaged in the... uh, crash," he said

sheepishly.

"Really? Then 'crash' was no overstatement?" Lily asked.

"Um, certainly not," Andrew said.

"Andrew, *shhhh*," Brick said with a smile.

Lily shook her head. "Then I have no way of giving even an approximate date, especially considering I was not present for its discovery."

"But this language is a dead language, is it not?" Brannigan asked.

She nodded. "It is indeed."

"Then could that not be seen as one means of dating?"

Lily nodded again. "In some fashion, but another wrench in the works is that onyx would not have been readily available in Sumer to have made this–if we are assuming it was made in Sumer at all."

"If not Sumer," Brannigan said. "Then where?"

"I have no idea. But if we hope to discover where and when this was created," Lily said, "I suggest we decode it as quickly as possible. I think you would agree, Hugo, that after our altercation with the German troops today, time is certainly of the essence."

Silently, Brannigan nodded.

***

"*Dead*?"

"Yes, Herr Delacroix, the soldiers are dead."

"I am bloody glad they were your men, Von Faust, and not *mine*."

189

Black Fang Delacroix was standing on a balcony overlooking Tangier's tangled medina as the sun descended over the ocean to the west.

"But we were correct in assuming Brannigan would come to Tangier," Von Faust said.

"No, Monsieur," Fang said, frowning. "*I* was correct in that supposition. You have been correct about very little in recent time."

Von Faust squirmed under Fang's gaze. "Um. Perhaps."

"What's next, Captain?" Fang asked, the threatening words of *der Klinge* ringing in his head. "I believe I was advised to heed *all* of your advice."

Von Faust paced back and forth, crossing his arms over his fascist medal-adorned chest. "We know he is in the medina," he said. "And we know he must be staying with friends."

"Yes, Captain. I know that. But as I said: what *now*?"

"Who are Brannigan's contacts in the city, Herr Delacroix? Can we find them–"

"We did that, Captain," Fang sighed. "We know of two contacts Brannigan has in the city: Monsieur Max and this mysterious *Le Duc*. Currently, my men are searching for this *Le Duc*, quite a reclusive figure he is. And we did locate Monsieur Max already, which was how we located Brannigan today. Unfortunately, *your men* did not capture Brannigan when they had the chance, despite his being trapped in a stone building."

Von Faust was apparently unbothered by his recent failings. "So... this *Le Duc*... how do we find him?"

"That I do not know," Fang said.

"Perhaps you should focus on that, Herr Delacroix,"

Von Faust said as he took a seat. From a pocket he pulled a pack of cigarettes and a swastika-engraved lighter. He leaned back and lit a cigarette. "Now?" he suggested.

Fang sighed. "Yes, Captain."

***

Night had fallen, the band was in full swing, the dance floor was filled with young men and women from around the world doing the Lindy Hop, and our adventurers were three cups of coffee in each and making breakthroughs!

On stage, six ladies dressed to dance ripped through a smoking version of "Sing, Sing, Sing" that would make even Benny Goodman jealous, the name stenciled on the bass drum head reading *THE BELLE HOPS*.

"That bird on the clarinet sure is a dish!" Andrew said, losing his focus for about the tenth time that evening.

"Andrew, if you want to dance, then go dance!" Brannigan said (also for about the tenth time).

"No, Professor! We've got work to do."

Point of fact, Lily was doing most of the work. Brannigan was acting as righteous moral support while Andrew was little more than a distraction.

"Actually, Andrew, I would be delighted if you took a break," Lily sighed.

"You got it, Doc!" The young man leapt from his seat as though it were spring-loaded. A moment later he was Lindy Hopping with a young local girl, a huge smile on his face.

"Are you all right, Lily?" Brick asked, genuinely concerned.

He was asking, you see, because things had stopped adding up. Dr. Halifax was shaking her head, currently baffled by the wholly anachronistic results she was finding.

"It just doesn't make sense, Hugo!"

"What, dear?"

"What the Cipher reads. I have no way of dating it, and what I'm translating doesn't make sense."

"Tell me," he said. "We will talk it out."

She turned the black disc to face him. "See this? This is referencing cultures and civilizations that had not yet existed until after the fall of Sumer!"

Brannigan chewed his lip. "Example?" he said.

"It mentions Babylonia here, which was essentially the successor to Sumer. But it also mentions the Hittites–who came later, the Minoans–who were on a different continent, the Phoenicians–who came later, the Mayans–who were on the other side of the Atlantic, and even the Romans and Byzantines. This doesn't make any sense!"

"Unless it was made later, correct?"

"Certainly, but who would make a Cipher later in a such an extinct language?"

"Someone trying to protect a secret," Brannigan suggested. "This is exactly what Dr. Spooner believed!"

"What do you mean?"

"Ellis suggested that there would be one key relic that could act as a map to find the others. He conjectured that this relic would hold clues as to where to find the other relics needed by the Cabal to fulfill their unholy right!"

"Ergo, we need to crack the Cipher first?"

"Yes, exactly!"

"And you believe this is it? This is *the* Cipher?" Lily's face was growing slightly pale.

"Yes! No doubt it works with the scroll Andrew and I liberated from Delhi. Damn my judgement in returning it to Branford," he muttered. "Anyway, are there any reference values included on the disc?"

"Reference values?"

"Yes, points from which we can derive directional or navigational coordinates! Cartesian, celestial, or otherwise! There were certain values on the scroll, but they seemed... far too random to be random!" Brannigan was growing excited, and Lily could not help but feel it, as well.

"As a matter of fact, there are. Just another thing that has been confusing me, considering–"

"Ahaha! Brilliant! They must go together! Why, you clever girl! Complimentary values! That is just brilliant!" Brannigan slapped his hand down on the table, rattling the dishes.

Lily laughed. "I'm glad you are so excited, Hugo. What do we do now?"

He stood. "We celebrate! This is a remarkable discovery that will hopefully help save the world!"

"What? Celebrate did you say? How?"

The Belle Hops finished the extended "Sing, Sing, Sing" to thunderous applause. Sweating and smiling, the trumpet player approached the microphone. "*C'est une chanson qui sera bientôt enregistré par notre ami* Django Reinhardt. *Jouir de.*"

The lovely Belle Hops kicked up a swinging version of a song (as yet unrecorded), soon to be known as "Minor Swing." Brannigan, smiling, took Lily's hand and led her to the dance floor.

They sure showed those kids how it was done. If they can save the world, you're damn right they can swing dance.

***

When the band packed up, the dancers departed, and *le Fugitif* was quiet, Brannigan, Lily, and Andrew headed upstairs. Our adventurers were tired–understandably–and they had a big day ahead of them. Brannigan carried the Cipher and Mortimer's text (which had yet to be consulted due to persistently wet pages) in one hand, his other rested on Lily's shoulder.

"You are a wonderful dancer, Hugo," Lily said. "Very... spirited!" She was sweaty and exhausted, but she could not remember having a better night. "I will have to thank Miette again, it was a glorious evening."

"We will thank her, dear. But I must say, you are a marvel on the dance floor. You know, at Branford I used to chaperone dances on Friday and Saturday nights. Wanda would also chaperone and she taught me to dance. Chaperoning is much more enjoyable when you've someone to dance with," he smiled.

"Wanda?" Lily asked, eyebrows raised. "Wanda *Bullington*? Quincy's secretary?"

"She's a good friend, dear, that's all!" he smiled and laughed.

"I'd hope so! She's twice your age!"

"But can that old bird dance," he smiled again.

Upstairs, they found Nero leaning back in a chaise

lounge, eyes at half mast. In one hand was the coiled cord to the telephone that he twisted absently.

"Archibald," Lily asked. "Are you feeling any better? You looked dreadful earlier."

Nero looked up, his face pale, his eyes blank. "Oh. Yes. I feel much better, Liliana. Thank you."

"Are you sure, old chap?" Brannigan asked. "Why aren't you sleeping? I helped you to bed earlier, after all."

"You did, Hugo," Nero said. "But I could not sleep."

"Well, you better try," Brannigan said. "I need you rested for tomorrow. Tomorrow you're going to fly us out of here."

Nero nodded. "That will be no problem," he said, his voice cold.

Brannigan wrapped one arm around Lily's waist and pulled her close to him. "I hope not," he said. "So get some rest, eh?"

Nero only nodded and stared off into space. Had Brannigan and Lily been more focused, perhaps they would have noticed something wrong. Unfortunately, they did not.

Instead, they adjourned to the balcony. "I have something to show you," Brick said.

Outside, the sky was a marvelous midnight blue flecked by an infinite number of perfect stars. *Le Fugitifi* was thankfully tall enough to get its balcony up over the roofs of most other buildings in the medina, so even from their vantage on the balcony, Brick and Lily could see the Strait of Gibraltar perfectly. He stood behind her, wrapped one arm around her waist, and pointed with the other.

In the distance, a clear white light blinked slowly.

"You see that?" Brick said.

"Yes, darling."

"That is the Europa Point Lighthouse at the very tip of the Iberian Peninsula. A very good friend of mine operates that old lighthouse. That is Spain. Have you ever been to Spain?"

"Never," she said.

He smiled. "I will take you. Spain is one of the most romantic places in all the world, but never have I had the opportunity to explore it with someone before. Until now."

She turned and kissed him. "I can't wait," she said.

Under the stars, they kissed. It was perhaps the most perfect ending to the most perfect evening. Neither Brick nor Lily could remember feeling so happy.

Unfortunately for our intrepid hero and heroine, things were about to change...

CHAPTER 25: Bullets in the Night–and a Terrible Madness Seizes One of Our Heroes! (Fear Not, Dear Reader, For There Will Always Be Hope Where Brick Brannigan is Involved!)

Gunfire awoke Dr. Liliana Halifax whilst in mid-dream. It was a wonderfully pleasant dream after a wonderfully pleasant evening. Unfortunately, she woke into a nightmare.

Voices shouted in German, and the gunfire was only matched in sound by the shattering of glass. Lily stumbled out from under her blankets in her bedclothes and raced to the door. Unlocking it, she pulled it open a crack.

In the hall, Brick and Andrew were kneeling together behind an overturned table, firing shots from a pair of revolvers.

"Get Nero!" Brannigan shouted. "We have to go!"

"Aye, Professor!"

The heavy *BOOMBOOMBOOM* of a rifle shook the very walls of the rooms above *le Fugitif*, and Lily closed her doors and snatched up her belongings. In a moment, she was dressed and ready. She pulled a bag over her shoulder and stuffed the Cipher inside it along with her copious notes and Mortimer's slim text. Once more, she opened the door.

"Lily! Lily get down!" Brannigan shouted.

Gunfire precluded him from saying more, but Lily withdrew enough to avoid the 30.06 slug that buried itself in her door frame with a splintering *crack*.

A moment later, Brannigan leapt across the narrow hall and into her room.

"Are you all right?" he asked, embracing her. "You weren't hit, were you?"

"No, no, I'm all right," she said, holding him tightly. "Are you okay?"

"I'm fine, I'm fine!"

"What's going on?"

"It's that Black Fang bastard," he said, grimacing. "He found me somehow. I'm sure Von Faust is here, as well."

"Who?"

"Trouble," Brannigan said as he walked to the door and fired a pistol shot into the ceiling lamp, dropping the hall into darkness. "Get ready, we'll need to leave quickly, my dear."

"I'm ready, Hugo," she said, pulling the strap of her shoulder bag tight.

The great adventurer smiled. "You are indeed."

Somewhere below them, the mad gatling-like report of twin Tommy guns came to life and Brannigan could not help but laugh.

"They've woken Miette," he said. "God help them."

"What's the plan?"

"Get Nero up and get the hell out of here. Andrew is rousting the surly Brit now."

As if on cue, a voice echoed down the hall. "What the devil is happening, Brannigan?"

"Black Fang's welcoming party, Nero," Brick said with a smile.

"Am I supposed to know who that is?" Nero asked from the adjacent doorway.

Brannigan frowned. "Of course, Nero. We had a run-in with him in Alice Springs last summer. He's got black teeth?"

"Oh, yes. Black Fang Delacroix. How could I have forgotten?"

Brannigan turned a worried eye to Lily. "I hope he's well enough to fly," he said. "I don't think I've it in me to get that bird off the ground again alone."

Lily took his hand. "We will make it."

He smiled. "You're right. We will."

Frantic German shouting interrupted our brave adventurers as Miette arrived. .45 slugs ripped through the subdued wallpaper and walls, leaving nothing but dust and dead soldiers in the tumultuous wake. For a moment, all was silent.

"Hugo? Lily? *Vous êtes en vie, non*?"

"We are," Brannigan and Lily said at once as they came out from cover.

Miette stood barefoot in the hall in a surprisingly short silk nightgown, her two machine guns on her hips, muzzles pointed up at the bullet-ridden ceiling. Smoke curled from each barrel.

"I tire of asking such questions," Miette sighed. "What of the boy? And your *amour-frappé ami*?"

"Andrew is well. Nero is sick, but alive."

"I am fine, Brannigan," Nero said, his voice still oddly cold and hollow.

"*Voulez-vous me baiser, cochon*?" she asked Nero.

"What is this Frenchwoman saying?" Nero asked.

Sharing a look, Brannigan and Lily both said, "He is definitely sick."

"Miette," Brannigan said after a humorous moment. "We need to leave quickly. What have you got?"

"I have a pair of Ariel Red Hunters. They are in the back. Take them if you need. But, Hugo, *si vous avez un accident eux, Je vais vous trouver.*"

"We will take good care of them, Miette," Brannigan said with a grin. "You have my word."

"Red Hunters?" Lily asked with a raised eyebrow.

Brannigan smiled. "Motorcycles."

"Oh dear," Lily said with a frown.

***

Brannigan and Lily rode one Red Hunter, Nero and Andrew the second. The revving of engines was incredibly loud in the tight confines of the medina, but the sound was almost lost in the shrieking of Miette's machine guns.

"Will she be all right?" Lily asked as they took off.

Brannigan shouted back to her, "Miette could destroy a whole army single-handedly. I have never worried for her safety. I worry more for the total destruction of all of Tangier by her hand!"

The two bikes sped through the narrow streets, thankfully empty in the early morning hours. Up and down the cobblestone passages they raced, bouncing and jostling over the rough roadway. A few store owners were turning on lights as the motorcycles rushed past, the machines casting clouds of exhaust and dust up into the air.

Brannigan led the way. Behind him, Nero steered perfectly, his illness not seeming to hinder his driving ability one iota. Seeing such skill, Brannigan could do nothing but breathe a sigh of relief. *If Nero can fly*, he thought, *we have a chance of getting out of here*!

It wasn't long before rays of sun began reaching down into the alleyways and the sound of their pursuit became more evident. When the two motorcycles exploded from the suffocating confines of the medina and onto the wide roadways leading to the airstrip, a pair of Alfa Romero roadsters closed in on their tails.

"You're going to have to shoot!" Brannigan shouted to Lily.

"Shoot what?"

"There's a pistol," he hollered, "in my belt!"

To herself more than anyone, Lily said, "Oh my."

With both arms already wrapped around Brannigan's substantial chest, she lowered one very carefully until she felt the grip in her hand. She pulled it free and turned to look over her shoulder.

One of the black roadsters was closer than she thought, perhaps only ten or so yards from their rear wheel. Twisting in the seat, she raised the barrel over her shoulder and took aim.

Before she could fire, rapid machine gun fire exploded from the second roadster. Brannigan and Nero–now driving side-by-side–swerved as bullets raked across the asphalt.

"They're going for our tires!" Brannigan shouted.

201

"Aim for theirs! We're in trouble if we can't lose them!"

Even as he spoke, he twisted the bike to the right, steering it off the main road and onto a narrower side street. Nero shadowed him perfectly the whole way.

Behind them, the roadster drivers were not quite so skilled. The black car made the turn just in time, taking out a collection of roadsigns, but continuing nonetheless. His partner swerved too late and collided with a parked lorry in a flurry of sparks and a grinding of metal.

Brannigan let rip a victorious laugh as Lily opened fire on the remaining roadster.

The pistol in her hand was heavy and had a good kick, so the first two shots were wasted. The third hit the car's hood, making a two inch wide hole in the metal. The fourth shot cracked the windshield.

Watching in his rearview, Brannigan shouted, "That's it, my love!"

Did he say 'love'? Lily thought, even as she squeezed off the fifth shot. *This Brannigan character sure moves fast!* Distracted as she was, you can understand why the fifth shot missed.

"I think he did say love," she said aloud to herself as she took fresh aim.

"What did you say, my darling?" Brannigan shouted.

"Nothing!"

She smiled as she took the sixth and final shot. The bullet connected with the driver's side front tire and the rubber tubing exploded. Struggle as he may to maintain control, the unfortunate driver failed. The Alfa Romero twisted and turned sharply, flipping as it left the roadway and crashed into an argan tree. A moment later, Brannigan watched in his mirror as the roadster went up in flames.

"Well done, Lily!" Brannigan shouted as the two motorcycles disappeared into the early morning traffic.

***

Alas for Miette, she had only a limited supply of ammunition. Were this not the case, surely the tiny, fierce Frenchwoman could conquer the world.

As it was, she did not. And when she ran out, Von Faust's men closed in.

She sat just off her dance floor in one of her cafe's chairs, hands tied behind her back. A black circle was forming around her left eye from where she was barbarously subdued by one of Von Faust's men. At the moment, a handful of German soldiers stalked around her like predatory cats.

"Clear the room," a voice said from the door.

Slowly, the German soldiers trickled out until only one man remained.

"*Bonjour*, Mademoiselle Tati. It has been... Three years? No?"

The Frenchwoman, gagged as she was, could not speak. Although it should be noted that had she not been gagged, she still would not have spoken. Frowned strenuously, perhaps.

Black Fang Delacroix walked into the room, one hand behind his back, one hand closed on the scimitar at his hip.

"Yes, three years, I believe. I must say, it is good not to be the only French fugitive in the room." He smiled his black-toothed smile. "You have done well for yourself."

Miette glared at Fang.

203

"I'm sorry your club has been... ruined. The name is not so clever, though." He smiled. "But appropriate."

He pulled an intact chair out from a mess of smashed furniture and placed it across from her. "Do you know why I am here, Mignonette?"

Perhaps only noticing the gag now, Fang reached out and untied it. Ungagged, Miette smiled and spat in his face.

"That does not answer my question," he said, wiping the spit away. "So I will assume the answer is no. I am here for the man you harbored. I am here for Brick Brannigan. You know him, yes?"

Miette did not reply.

"Unfortunately," Fang continued. "I know him quite well. He has proven quite a... thorn in my side."

Miette smiled once more.

"So you do know him?"

"I know Hugo, yes," she said. "I know not where he is or where he is going. Although I hope you find him..."

Fang raised his eyebrows. "Yes?"

"...so he can kill you, *merde dégoûtant*,"

"*Ne me parlez pas comme ça!*" Fang growled, standing quickly in anger. "*Tu veux que je te tue?*"

Miette smiled. "You will not kill me," she said.

"And why not?" Fang asked, his face red with fury.

"*Parce que... Le Duc.*"

"*Le Duc,*" Fang said. "I've heard much of this man. Who is he?"

"He is... *un prodige*," Miette said. "The Americans would call him a hero. And, though I need it not, I am under his protection."

Fang smiled. "I am protected by more than a myth," he said. "I have the might of the German army behind me. And unfortunately for your friends, I already know their plans. They stand no chance."

Miette smiled. "*Puis me tuez, vous lâche.*"

"I am no coward," Fang said.

He stood for a moment, thinking. Before you draw too many judgements, remember, dear reader, that Fang is a complicated man. It has been many years since he's enjoyed his work.

With a sigh, he glanced over his shoulder. The soldiers were milling outside. He could hear their voices, but not see them. He turned back to Miette.

"I'm sorry, Mignonette," he said softly. "*Je suis désolé.*"

From his belt he pulled a black revolver and cocked it.

Miette steeled herself. She would not beg. She would look down the barrel with dry eyes.

Fang took a step towards her and lashed out, pistol-whipping her across the temple with the revolver, overturning the chair. Miette collapsed to the floor, unconscious. "*Je suis désolé,*" he repeated. That done, he raised the pistol and fired one shot into the ceiling over his head. Dust rained down gently.

Black Fang Delacroix turned away from Miette and strode quickly from *le Fugitif*. Outside, a wave of soldiers approached.

"It is done," he said, halting their advance. "Time to go."

From the back of the crowd, a bald-headed man pushed to the front. "Go where?" Von Faust asked. "This was our only lead! You just killed our only source!"

Fang smiled his black-toothed smile. "Monsieur Von Faust," he said. "Did you not believe I had at least one ace up my sleeve?"

Dear reader, I have to say, his last smile was truly worrisome.

***

Nero's precious *Belladonna* took flight just as the sun lifted itself over the horizon. Destination: Ponta Delgada in the archipelago of the Azores.

In the cockpit, Nero sat behind the stick. To his right sat Andrew, watching cool blue ocean fall away beneath them. In the back, Brannigan sat on a jump seat beside Lily.

"I am almost sad to be going home," Lily said. "I feel like I just left Branford."

Brannigan smiled. "I told you, my dear, this is just the beginning. We need to take the Eye of Aja back to Quincy so we know it's safe. You can work with him to decipher whatever you have and match it to the scroll. When that is finished, we can set out once again."

"I like the sound of that. Spain, you said?"

"We will go to Spain, certainly. Perhaps we will visit Krakow first. Or Wellington. Or Cape Town. Or Moscow. Or Santiago. Or–"

"That's enough, that's enough," Lily laughed. "I get it. We can go anywhere."

"No, my dear. We will go *everywhere*. Our adventures are just beginning, and we are young. Remember, we've a world to save."

"How could I forget?"

Leaning together, they kissed.

Abruptly, he pulled away. "Oh, I meant to show you!"

Smiling, Lily rolled her eyes as he stood and rushed to the wall of the plane's fuselage. With a tug, he pulled a panel free, exposing wiring and cables beneath. Reaching his great arm inside, he withdrew what looked like... a skull.

"What is that?" Lily asked, grimacing as she rubbed her stomach.

"Why, it's what brought me to the Niger Delta, of course!"

He returned to his seat, carrying the skull. "It is the skull of a Clockwork Man, and if my theories are correct..."

His great hands moved over the rusty construct, testing each seam and screw head, searching for some hidden trick.

"What are you looking for, my dear?" Lily asked, her voice slightly pained.

"Just one more..." A finger pressed some hidden trigger and the skull in his hands opened with a pneumatic *hiss*. "Ahh, there!"

The robotic skull had opened in his hands, revealing inside a great gemstone unlike anything Lily had ever seen.

"My lord," she said, eyes wide. "That must be..."

"The Eye of Aja!" Brannigan smiled. "Yes, indeed!" He passed the remarkable stone to her. "As I said, darling, this is just the beginning!"

"So this and the Cipher..." she began, looking up at

Brannigan.

"I don't want to say *priceless*," he said. "But, yes, they are essentially priceless relics."

"And the Cabal wants them?"

He nodded. "Without a doubt." He looked at Lily and frowned. "Are you all right?"

She grimaced again. "My stomach," she said. "I feel ill."

"Airsick?"

"Perhaps, but it's never happened before." Slowly, she stood. "I need to use the lavatory."

She took a half-dozen unsteady steps with Brannigan a few paces behind before she collapsed to her knees and retched onto the bare floor of the airplane.

"Lily!" Brannigan said, kneeling at her side.

She shook her head repeatedly and motioned him away. Brannigan nodded and acquiesced.

When she had finished, she leaned back. "Oh my," she said. "I feel better..." she trailed off.

"You do?" There was a long silence. "Lily?"

"Hugo," she said softly. "What is this?"

Brannigan walked quickly to her side. There on the deck amidst little more than water and stomach acid was a worm, long and black.

"Wings of Icarus," he said. "That's... that's impossible!"

"What is it?" Lily asked, suddenly frightened.

"It can't be..." he said softly.

"Hugo, what is it? You're scaring me!"

He was at her side in a moment. "I'm sorry, sweet

ladybird. You are all right; you are safe. I promise you that you are okay. As for the rest of us..." He shook his head. "That is something called a... Vøttur worm."

"A what?"

"It's rare, terribly rare. It's from the Faroe Islands. 'Vøttur' means 'glove.' They travel in... *ice*. It's... it's a parasite that can be controlled by special electrodes..."

"Controlled? Hugo, you're frightening me..."

He shook his head. "We're in trouble," he said.

Suddenly, the aircraft shuddered unnaturally, forcing Brannigan to wrap a protective arm around Lily.

"What was that?" she asked. "What's going on?"

"I don't know," he said. "But do you feel that? We're turning."

"What?"

"Turning... *east*. Something's wrong."

Brannigan was beginning to understand, but it was too late. Unsteady on the moving aircraft, he rushed to the cockpit and banged open the door.

The first thing he saw was Andrew, unconscious. A goose egg was forming on his forehead from where he'd been hit with some blunt object. The second thing he saw was Nero on the radio, speaking... *German*.

"*Geschätzte Zeit nach Berlin*," he said, checking his watch. "*Etwas mehr als 24 stunden*."

Brannigan's German was truly awful, but he understood well enough. From Nero's words, Brannigan understood: something something *Berlin* something something *24 hours*. Even butchered as that translation was, Brannigan realized it couldn't be good!

"Berlin?" Brannigan said. "How could I have been so

foolish!"

From the depth of the plane, Lily raced. "Hugo!" she said. "What's going on? Why have we turned?"

Standing behind him, she stared at Nero. His face was deathly pale, his eyes dark and sunken in. He turned to look at them over his shoulder. "You were a fool, Brannigan!" he hissed in a voice not his own. "And now you will pay the price!"

"My God, Hugo! Nero's a Nazi?"

"No, Lily," Brannigan said, taking a step back. "The worm, the Vøttur worm?" he shook his head. "I should have seen the symptoms! Damnit, Brannigan! Think, you fool!"

"Hugo, stop." Lily took his arm and turned him towards her. "Tell me, and we will work it out."

The fear that had bloomed in his chest dissipated, and he nodded. "You're right," he said. "You're right."

"The worm..." she prompted.

"Yes. The Vøttur worm is wholly parasitic. When not in a host, it must live in ice. Now that it has entered the game, I see that the symptoms were present for a while. You and Nero must have both been infected by the worm when you were moved from Port Harcourt to Tangier. Someone put the worm into the ice, do you see? It interfered with your resuscitation, that's why you almost did not revive. Your system was fighting the worm. Nero had no problem because his system accepted the worm. It all makes sense!"

"And this worm..."

"It effects... well, a sort of *mind control*!"

"My lord!" Lily said. "And so Nero?"

"He is being controlled by Von Faust! Or Black Fang Delacroix!"

"The men who attacked *le Fugitif*?"

"Yes, exactly!"

"And he is taking us to Berlin?"

Brannigan nodded. "Aye, to Berlin."

At this moment, when our seemingly bravest of heroes–Brick Brannigan–was lost to act, we are grateful, dear reader, to have such a remarkable heroine to step in and take his place!

From Brannigan's rucksack she pulled a pistol and raised it into the air. "Not if I can help it!" she said.

CHAPTER 26: For Everything That Begins, There Must Be an Ending (And For Everything That Ends, There is the Promise of a New Beginning)

Lily leveled the pistol at Nero's temple. "Turn this plane around, Archibald," she said.

"Archibald is not here right now," Nero's unnatural voice grated. "You are only here with *me* now."

Lily tightened her finger on the trigger. "Turn this plane around or I will kill you, whoever you are."

The face that was looking less and less like Nero with each passing moment turned towards Lily once more. "Then you must kill me, because as long as I live this plane will never change course."

Lily bit her lip and tightened her finger on the trigger.

"Oh who the hell am I kidding?" she said. "I'm an adventuress and a heroine, but I'm no murderer. And somewhere in there Archibald Nero still lives." She lowered the pistol.

"Unfortunately, you're right," Brannigan said. "But we've another option."

"And what is that?"

"Not to be on the plane when it arrives in Berlin."

"Not to be... Um, Hugo, dear, we're thousands of feet

212

in the air!"

Brannigan laughed and led her away from Zombie Nero towards the hold. He pulled open a crate and lifted three jungle green backpacks.

"And those are?"

"Parachutes!" Brannigan exclaimed.

"Oh my."

Quickly, he pulled a parachute onto Lily's back and fastened the harness.

"One for you, dear, one for me, and one for Andrew–if I can wake him in time. If not, I'll take him with me. It's all right, I've done this before. I'm sorry, I was rattled earlier, but I'm all right now. I'm back."

Lily smiled. "As am I. I'm worried about Archibald, though."

Brannigan shook his head. "The effects of the Vøttur are only temporary. After four or five days, the worm dies. Unfortunately, that is too long for us right now. Nero will come out of it. Soon enough, he'll be back to his foolish old self!"

"I hope so."

"But for now..."

A gunshot echoed throughout the plane. Brannigan pushed Lily behind him as he turned. Zombie Nero stood in the door to the cockpit, a pistol in his hand.

"Who's flying the plane?" Brannigan shouted.

"The autopilot."

"This plane has autopilot?" Brannigan hollered. "Why the hell didn't *I* know that? And I flew here all the way from–"

Another warning shot silenced him.

"Put down those parachutes and get back in your seats," Zombie Nero said, aiming his pistol at Brannigan's heart. "You are both wanted in Berlin. My Master has not specified dead or alive." He smiled. "So I leave it up to you."

From Zombie Nero's perspective, Lily's pistol was hidden. She pressed against Brick's back, urging him forward. Brannigan took a step towards Zombie Nero, hands raised.

"All right," he said. "Calm down, all is well."

"I said put down the parachute, Dr. Halifax. I will not ask again."

"It's buckled," she said, stalling for time as Brannigan took another step towards Zombie Nero. "I... um... Darling can you help me with this?"

"Certainly!" Brannigan turned and as he did he ducked. Lily raised her pistol and fired.

Who's to say what she was aiming for, dear reader, but she missed Zombie Nero and instead put a .38 slug through the cockpit's windshield. The thick glass cracked ominously before exploding with a fierce *WHOOOSH* of air.

Brannigan rose and turned, lunging for Zombie Nero. The two collided as Nero's pistol fired up and into the ceiling.

Behind them, young Caine was awake and struggling from the cockpit, hands white-knuckled against the interior as he pulled himself from the cockpit.

Brannigan continued battling with Zombie Nero, the once British pilot now apparently blessed with superhuman strength as well as malice.

Lily rushed to their bags. From within Brannigan's

rucksack she pulled his old leather satchel. She jammed the Eye of Aja back into the mechanical skull and stuffed the whole thing inside. Fighting against the sucking wind, she struggled to the fuselage door and looked out the window.

Below she saw only the crisp blue of the Mediterranean sea.

"No!" Brannigan shouted. "Wait! We need to get over land or we've no chance!"

Crawling on all fours (now wearing both the parachute and Brannigan's satchel–packed to the gills) Lily slowly approached Brick and Nero, pistol in hand.

A few paces from them, she raised the pistol, leveling it at Zombie Nero's leg. Despite the rocking of the plane and the *roar* of wind, she locked her aim and fired.

The bullet sliced through Nero's calf just as planned. Zombie or no Zombie, Nero's leg buckled under his weight. Seizing the moment, Brannigan freed one hand from Nero's grasp and smashed it into the poor Zombie's face. A second and third shot followed before their friend was little more than a pile on the floor.

"Thank you, my dear!" Brannigan said as he crouched beside Lily. "Now get ready to jump!"

"But we're over water!"

"It's the Mediterranean. I twist that stick marginally and we'll be over solid ground in two shakes of a lamb's tail. Just be ready!"

He turned from her, preparing to descend into the hell that was the cockpit, when she stopped him with a hand on his arm. He turned back to her.

"Be careful," she said. "Come back to me, all right?"

He smiled. "I will always come back, I promise."

She hugged him, an air of desperation in her grasp. When they separated, he looked into her beautiful eyes and said, "You know, I think I may love you, Liliana!"

She flushed and kissed him. "And I just may love you, Hugo!"

He could not help but grin like a fool before saying, "I'll be right back!"

Carefully, he turned from her, seized two parachutes from the floor, and began crawling back towards the cockpit, the fierce air tugging at him stronger with every pace.

Just outside the cockpit, he passed young Caine the parachute and pushed him back towards the fuselage door. "Take care of her," he said. "When you hear me shout, you open that door and jump, you hear?"

Andrew nodded.

"I'll be right behind you!"

Andrew crawled back to Lily and shouted minimal parachute instructions to her before he took his place at the door. He watched as the Professor disappeared into the cockpit. Almost immediately, Lily could feel the plane bank to the left as their course changed from Northeast to Northwest.

"We have to wait," she said. "Hugo will be back! He will go with us!"

Andrew nodded. "Stay close to me," he said. "When the Professor gives me the signal, he said to open this door and jump. He'll be right behind."

"No," she said. "We have to wait for him."

"I do what the Professor tells me, Doctor!"

Scowling, Lily said, "Yes, but I have the pistol!"

216

"Okay!" Andrew said. "We can wait!"

A moment later, Brannigan's form appeared in the cockpit doorway. He waved his arms at young Caine, shouting, "Now! Open the door! Now!"

Lily looked outside and saw sandy beaches below.

Young Caine turned a questioning eye to her.

"We wait," she said.

Behind her, Brannigan continued shouting. "Now!" he pleaded. "Go now!" He slipped back into the cockpit to correct course.

"We need to go, Doctor!" Andrew shouted.

"No!" Lily insisted. "We wait!"

Behind them, Zombie Nero had stirred. Without anyone noticing, he had begun climbing to his feet. Blood poured from his leg wound, but he seemed neither to notice nor care. Upright, he turned and began stalking towards Lily and Andrew.

"He said to go, Doctor! And I listen to the Professor!"

"I won't leave him!" Lily said.

"He'll be right... *BEHIND YOU*!"

Lily turned as Zombie Nero closed two hands around her throat. "No!"

Andrew released the door and leapt at Nero, clawing at his face and striking his body. The blows were ineffectual against the possessed Brit.

From the cockpit, Brannigan emerged, hair tussling wildly in the wind.

"Lily!" he shouted.

In a flash, he crossed the body of the plane–he has nigh preternatural abilities, remember?–and tackled Zombie Nero, wrenching his hands from off Lily's neck. She scrambled away from them, gasping for breath.

Andrew pulled her towards him. "Are you all right, Doctor?"

She nodded, unable to speak, only able to watch.

Brannigan dragged Zombie Nero away from his friends, battling the possessed beast each step of the way. Outside the cockpit, he turned, gazing at the control panel.

"We're losing altitude," he shouted to Andrew. "You must go now!"

"Doctor," Andrew said to Lily.

Still unable to speak, she only shook her head.

"Andrew!" Brannigan said. "Do it now! Take Dr. Halifax... or all will be lost!"

Young Caine nodded and turned the lever, releasing the fuselage door. The great metal hatch opened and was ripped from the plane by the searing wind.

Lily shook her head madly as Andrew knelt at her side.

"I'm sorry, Doctor. Remember what I told you? And remember to roll when you land."

He seized her shoulder strap and pulled, dragging her unwilling body over the threshold and out of the plane. At the last minute, her throat cleared and she shouted, "Hugo!"

Then she was gone.

Young Caine turned back. Brannigan still battled Nero, two giants locked in a life or death struggle.

"Go, lad! I will... find you! I promise!"

Only able to nod, Andrew gave his dear friend one last look and jumped.

Lily remembered all of Andrew's hurried instructions. She even rolled when she landed on the beach. She released the parachute and watched the wind pull it out over the water.

She was on wet sand. A few hundred yards away was a lighthouse.

Is that the Europa Point Lighthouse? she wondered. *Will Hugo take me to see it? Will I ever see Hugo again?*

She could not bear the thought. Throat aching after her struggle with Nero, she coughed and struggled for a deep breath as Andrew's parachute descended not far from where she stood. Tightening the shoulder strap of Brannigan's satchel that she yet carried, she rushed to him.

The young man was floundering in his parachute, apparently a less delicate lander than Lily herself. She cleared him from the tangles of the 'chute and helped him to his feet.

"I'm sorry, Dr. Halifax, I truly am. But the Professor–"

"It's all right, Andrew. You were right, as was he. I just... I couldn't..." She shook her head, unable to finish that sentence. "Anyway, now we must hurry. We have to see where Hugo lands."

The two adventurers turned. Together they watched Nero's precious *Belladonna* continue to lose altitude, occasionally shifting to the left or right as if control of the plane was still up for grabs.

"You didn't see the Professor jump already, Miss?"

Lily shook her head. "Not yet." The plane continued to descend. "Jump, Hugo," Lily whispered. "Please."

It turned due west, moving out to sea. From her vantage, Lily could see black ships setting out from the coast.

"Good lord," she said. "Those must be the Cabal. Get out of there Hugo!"

Still the plane lost altitude. The distance between the plummeting aircraft and the azure Mediterranean was closing far too quickly. But there was a chance, wasn't there? Brannigan himself would say there's always a chance!

Both our brave adventurers were watching when the plane hit the Mediterranean with a terrible crash. Jets of water exploded into the air, heralding its landing.

Lily covered her mouth. "Oh no," she said.

Andrew could not believe it. He only shook his head and said, "Professor?"

A long moment passed as Lily contemplated her past and future, perhaps even her fate. Was Brick Brannigan dead? Would she be left wondering, searching the deepest reaches of the ocean for sign of her love's life or death?

No, she would not. For you see, dear reader, Liliana Halifax knew beyond a shadow of a doubt that Brick Brannigan did yet live. To her, it was nothing short of a certainty. It was not a question of whether he lived or not, only a question of when she would see him again. For those ships belonged to the Cabal, and at this point her love was tightly in their grasp. The only thing left to do was save him, of course. She had the Cipher, the Eye of Aja, a pistol, and a daring assistant.

More importantly, she had the fierce adventuress blood. And there was nothing that could stop her.

"Come on, Andrew," she said, grabbing the young lad's

arm. "We have to go."

Dazed, the young man said, "What? Go where?"

"Away from the beach," Lily said. "The Cabal most certainly saw our 'chutes. They will come searching for us. I have the Cipher and the Eye, and neither can fall into their grasp. We need to get to safety and regroup."

"Regroup for what, Doctor?"

"For what comes next," she said with a resilient smile. "We're going to save Hugo." She looked at the distant lighthouse. *We're going to come for you, my love. We will find you, I promise.*

Young Caine turned to her, his spirits buoyed, and smiled. "And then?" he asked.

Lily laughed. "Why, save the world, of course!"

EPILOGUE

As Drs. Brannigan and Halifax were plummeting from the sky, and Black Fang Delacroix was setting sail on an appropriately black cutter for the Strait of Gibraltar, one Monsieur *Le Duc* was exiting a certain nightclub in Tangier after having attended to young firebrand Mignonette Tati.

A barrel-chested man with an extraordinarily terrible temper, Monsieur *Le Duc* generally contented himself in drinking absinthe in the company of beautiful women (purportedly two or three at once; he was a *prodige* in more ways than one) and opining on the troubling state of Dadaism and the neglected dangers a certain young Austrian *provocateur* posed in the tumultuous sea of German politics. It certainly took a great deal for Monsieur *Le Duc* to involve himself in the business of others, but after visiting Mademoiselle Tati, it became evident to the great man that the time for hesitation was through.

***

Do not fear for Professor Brannigan, dear reader, for Dr. Halifax has enough hope in her heart to carry us all through even the darkest of times. There is no one I would rather rely upon than her. And because of that...

Brick Brannigan will return...

in

BRICK BRANNIGAN IS BURIED ALIVE ON THE FAROE ISLANDS!

ABOUT THE AUTHOR!

Eric Bonkowski lives in Delaware. He is inspired daily by Saturday afternoon cliffhanger serials, classic comics and comic strips, and horror films of the '30s and '40s--to say nothing of mystery, fantasy, and science fiction pulp writings of every age.

He spends his time reading, watching campy movies, and writing, supported all the while by his remarkable wife and family. During the rare quieter moments, he can be found listening to jazz and falling asleep well before bedtime.

He is the author of the *Gil's Grimoire* series and the *Brick Brannigan* series.

Visit him at:

http://www.gilsgrimoire.com

http://www.brickbrannigan.com

www.ingramcontent.com/pod-product-compliance
Lightning Source LLC
Chambersburg PA
CBHW020407180626
46812CB00003B/864